The Third Step:
The Smoking Gun and the COUGHING NAILS, a Real Read Herring

the Isometrics of Tobacco and Power of Nonsense

By Al Lucas

DIAMOND MEDIA PRESS CO.
1-304-273-6157
https://www.diamondmediapressco.com/

Copyright © 2020
By Al Lucas
All rights reserved.

ISBN Paperback: 978-1-951302-57-3

Contents

The Compulsion

His garb was translucent; his soul, impeccable. He looked good outside; but inside, there was a barking need. It was the dog. The dog of doggerel. By all outward appearances, no one could tell what darkness intruded on his landscape. All he wanted was his words to soothe, his prose to tell a story, his story. However, it was more than a story. It was to be a saga of nicotine addiction.

Paul had just gotten out of jail on a pedophilia charge and was now doing time living a life of free will. His choice was to live for his cigarettes. When would he find God? In his spare time, which incidentally, abounded?

Zeus knew, but he was a Greek god. What good was he? He was fighting old wars. No degree, no order of higher speculation, no realization could possibly combat what Paul was dealing with. The real issue was his body; it was being defiled. Of course, there is such a thing as natural deterioration, but willful destruction no matter how incidental was immoral. Ah, the determinants of tar and a thousand other ingredients. There was also the specter of a sudden heart attack, an unpleasant reality for the best of us.

In essence, smoking was bad for you, in rumor and in fact.

But there was hope. Two-fold hope: one, modern science; and two, spiritual transfiguration. Both offered time: one, computerized; the other, transcendental. But life itself incorporates, integrates, and swallows. It is all consuming. Paul was bound and determined to defy the odds, and prick his conscience toward a resolution of some sort, i.e., quit somehow.

He had twelve years of recovery under his belt. But that was from alcohol. Twelve fucking years! Never mind what he was doing before, he was as spiritually fit as man could be considering his cigarette habit. He couldn't imagine giving up before leaving an imprint on the sand. He had already stepped all over his own ghastly accomplishments, trudging them into shadowy footprints, which no one in his right mind would follow.

Paul was continuing to do wrong. It was pleasing to his discomforted mind, and to a certain extent, pleasing to the rest of him to destroy himself. No need to go into medical detail, he was smoking. Right down to the butt. He felt the need for intervention: a new set of lungs, and, perhaps, a new rewired brain. Then he might be able to help rather than harm himself.

Theoretically, he could quit and exercise—rebuild the heart and lung—but that was doing it the hard way. He simply could not give up. He wasn't built that way. Presentiment supposed an ability to quit, but for Paul, it approached the impossible.

His only hope now was to postpone the inevitable and make a mark before an egregious exit was had. He had to tell his story. If only one person liked it, that would be enough. It would explain everything. But before the story begins, there is the Man.

And the only one man out there who had all the answers was Dr. Saw, noted brain surgeon, cardiologist and pulmonary expert, a body swapper of rare skill. But more of him later. Paul thought he must re-examine the body politic and the mind politic, two fronts constantly changing, and the craving, that driving force which transpires to make the urge come full bore on both sides. The body politic was to feel the pain and the pleasure; the mind politic, to follow the body. The dilemma was that the driving compulsion coupled with a defeating perception that it was fruitless to fight it made for a real showdown.

What identity did he want for himself? A goodie two shoes non-smoker or a hacker? He had been a personal failure up to now on many fronts so that identity was secure. He was a loser. Why change the dynamics so late in life? Why not just burn up the remaining years and let them extinguish into ash?

Dr. Saw might operate on him to save the day; but then again, Paul wanted to avoid the excoriation of skin and tissue by overcoming the impossible addiction and quit on his own will power, his mighty will power.

When is your quit date?

Not only would Paul not quit, he would not get involved in attempting to quit. Life without smoking was a waste. Life with smoking was a waste too.

So, it was a tie.

A Lucky Strike

He huffed and he puffed. He pulled, as they say in certain circles. The buildup of plague was more than subjective. So why worry? That was strictly subjective. Many a tribal woodsman had smoked until his eighties, his nineties; even centurions had been known to smoke happily until the end.

Why worry? That was too much subjectivity. The data accumulated indicated smoking was bad for your health. One wag had said, "ashes to ashes." Legions have died of lung cancer. Many a stroke or outright heart attack was attributable to the smoke. It was directly attributable, linked statistically and realistically, to puffing. Yet nothing smells better than a whiff of good South Carolina tobacco. That first hit always hits the spot. The nausea of twenty cigarettes is nothing compared to the cost. A pack goes for six dollars on average. That comes out for twenty cigarettes, or thirty cents a stick.

Doctor Saw seemed to be the only outlet. Preventative measures are far less expensive than last minute operations. Yet here was an operation that might be curative or postponing, to say the least. Doctor Saw could possibly, just possibly, but with no guarantees, save the day.

Herein lay the beef: he had only heard of Doctor Saw by word of mouth. Dr. Saw was sort of an iconic legend in the greater Tampa Bay area. He had performed medical miracles in his forty years of practice but had been banned from practice because of unorthodox procedures. He was a homeopath and an allopath. He was heroic in medical terms.

Paul unwrapped a box of his favorites, Lucky Strikes. He took one, non-filter of course, and lit up. Oh, how sweet it was. He looked at the back of the pack. Nestled behind the plastic wrap was a coupon.

He could hardly believe it. A photo of the renowned head of Dr. Saw stared him in the face. Over his dome read 'You're a Winner,' and a phone number in bold print.

That called for another cigarette. Perhaps this was his lucky day.

He called the number on the pack. "Hello?"

"Yes?" came a clipped response.

"I'd like to make an appointment with Dr. Saw."

When asked if he had insurance, Paul mused as he gazed up towards the ceiling, replying, "I want to pay in cash. I'm good for it."

"Bring a hundred thousand in twenties."

"Too much," Paul said, confusing his party with slang.

"Does that mean what I think it does?"

"It does. Who are you, by the way?" he interjected.

"Nurse Bite, compatriot of Dr. Saw."

He paused, eyeing his computer, and gave a short chuckle. "I'm Paul Undres, protagonist and anti-hero. I expose the ills of the world."

"What do you really want, Mr. Undres? A story or an operation?"

"I want a new set of lungs, one reprogrammed brain, and… a warranty," replied Paul.

A low whistle. "There are no guarantees in life."

"I want a product that will not fail."

"Tsk, tsk, tsk," Nurse Bite twittered.

Paul didn't seem to not have heard. "I want to breathe again, to feel the earth, the sun, and the wind."

"I see."

"The coupon on my Lucky's pack says I am a winner."

"You are indeed. He's quite good. He honors other people's brands too."

"Let's do it, Nurse Bite."

In a flat tone and a forced chuckle, she said, "Bring in the coupon."

Prepping

The first thing required of Paul was a laxative. He needed to purge his system of all free radicals. The second was a large dose of antioxidants. The third was an exhilarating nap of homeopathic dreams. Holistic he was.

Rested, he was ready.

But one question remained. How to locate Dr. Saw? Paul knew Tampa like the back of his hand, but the clandestine body part shack was not part of his geography. He called his AA friend, a former member of the Russian mafia.

"Karl, where is the location of Comrade Saw's shack?" asked Paul as he dabbed a bed of perspiration from his forehead.

"He is blackballed from our world, Paul."

"He still works. He's still advertising. You're out of touch, Karl," Paul said. "Where have you been?"

"Fermenting trouble. The U.S. is seeking to reestablish relations with Cuba. We need to maintain our drug channels. Need some dope?"

"I've got the shits, Karl," he grunted.

"Try some pain killers, that'll stop you up."

"I'll deal with you later."

An odd thought occurred to him. He immediately got on another line. "Tolstoy."

"Yes."

"Paul here. I've got a story for you."

A deep sigh could be heard coming from the other line. "None of this aristocratic nonsense, I hope."

"I want to find the location of Comrade Saw."

"The body part trafficker?"

"The very one, "

"He's in Cuba."

"I thought he was in Tampa?"

"Little Cuba, Ybor City."

"Oh, the Cigar City?" clarified Paul.

"Yes."

"But where?"

"Let me look up on Google Maps." A moment of silence passed. Then, an address was given. "7196 East Bank Drive."

"That's the place next to mine!" Paul exclaimed. "He's right under my nose!"

"He gets his mail there. Go next door and ask his stoolie."

"Got it."

His stoolie. The coincidences were getting too close for comfort. First the coupon, now this. He coughed up some phlegm. It was yellow, not a good sign. He felt the breath crushed from his lungs. Unfazed, he snapped his head back, exhaling slowly. He decided to go next door tomorrow. Right now, he needed to resuscitate. He would chill with another snooze and breathe on.

Life, after all, was a wheeze.

Daydreaming

IT WAS FAR AWAY— the calling, the wails, the cries of pain and suffering.

suffering. The world was hurting. The sounds got closer. A girl was knocking on his bedside window. She wanted his Yamaha synthesizer to hock. She had fucked his eyes out earlier in the day and needed more loving, this time, in the form of a dove, slang for a twenty piece. She wouldn't rest until she got her stone. Paul had already given her a twenty for her trouble and was in no mood to give her his cherished musical instrument.

The knocking was persistent. He shouted in his sleep, "Enough!" The spoken word carried power as the knocking abruptly stopped.

Crows descended. The cacophony was disturbingly pleasing. They were picking up the pieces of lint on the concrete parking lot. High above in the bright sun came these thoughts.

Paul, you will have a baby.

You're kidding!

He will be called Barabbas.

That's my nickname.

We thought it was fitting that someone so enamored with Biblical lore would have a baby that befitted his prejudices. You are a hater of self; so will your baby be.

I've been clean for twelve long fucking years. I'm not going to sacrifice all that for a child, and the womb that carries it."

You will become a transsexual via Dr. Saw then.

I want to be a lesbian. I hate men. They've been nothing but bores.

You are an operative man. You can hate the world.

Yes.

Sobering Thoughts

Paul awoke in a sweat. Where was he? He sat a moment in utter confusion. He looked out the window to verify his surroundings. The sun blinked to his stare. Everything seemed normal. Paul didn't want to become a transsexual. His mother and father taught him differently. Actually, they hadn't taught him a damn thing except to hit the books; but drugs undid all that.

So the brain is a resilient instrument, capable of great abuse and huge recovery. Like Medusa of lore, it fights back. If the snake bites, spit the venom out. Those crazy synapses will fire like mad when disturbed by poison. But life is not all reptilian, snake or no snake, mythical woman or no.

Life is a kaleidoscopic panorama of opportunity— and Paul partook it with as much zeal as his lungs would permit.

To get out of his death spiral required an uphill effort and a fighting spirit. Where in God's name would such a spirit come? It had to be Dr. Saw. He could not quit smoking. Nor was his general attitude the best. It was the consensus of all his beliefs that he needed to, but could not, would not even try.

He went next door.

"Yes?"

He didn't hate blacks. They were just too difficult to fathom. "I know you're a black man, a front for Dr. Saw. Care to tell me how to get into touch?"

The smug countenance of his neighbor brightened suddenly. "You know Saw?"

"He's an old friend."

"Have you got the coupon?" The man cocked his head to the side.

"Right here," replied Paul, nodding in acquiescence.

The man eyed him like a wary animal. "Go down Nebraska Avenue, past Lake. Ask for directions to the place called the Parts Shop."

"Thanks, bro."

"Why didn't you just call him and ask for directions?" The man's face hardened.

"Good question." With that, Paul let his footsteps echo behind him.

Dr. Saw

It was to be a do or die effort. Paul embarked in his trusty Prius determined to make the best of this opportunity. The traffic lights were all in his favor; the traffic flow cooperative. What he wanted was a real family doctor, someone who would explain the nature of his illness, and prescribe a home remedy that was holistic and defied accepted medical practice.

Dr. Saw was a body chopper, a Frankenstein of medicine. His procedures could hardly be deemed holistic. They were butchery with medical license. The normal response was not to try the unacceptable. He really had trouble facing what he was about to do. He was a naturalist, not a cyborg. He had no desire to become part man/part machine.

But look at the alternative— an unexpected clot that could paralyze half his body, leaving him staring vacantly for the rest of his life at the scenery, or a self-contained goon looking sadly at those he might or might not be able to recognize.

Hasty action might prove devastating. Instead, let the VA pay for a CAT scan to determine if he actually had cancer. As a 100 percent disabled veteran, he could afford it. A brain improperly programmed or an immune system that rejects its implant might cause more problems than simple paralysis. The scope of the problem was multifaceted. It was the big picture which needed looking into. What was right in God's eyes as opposed to human myopia?

The root of the problem was Paul liked the pleasure associated with puffing. The satiation of certain neurons from the smoke was satisfying and calming. The inhalation might be choking but was manageable. Good stuff was the smoke.

Chemicals, which kill everything in its path, were out. He would not do chemotherapy. He was clean from alcohol as he was a member of Alcohol Anonymous, and he would not tolerate any more poisons. Conversely, his outlook on life was meant to be taken slowly, puff by puff, coffee swig by coffee swig such was his addiction to those particular chemicals, which he granted were exceptional.

Basically, he had little patience for the temperate. He mocked them as they, him. He just didn't like do-gooders. But he was not a bad guy.

No, he was a good guy. Smoking was the one vice he had yet to overcome in the past or the present and would be the onus in the future. As an individual who mocked his own life and the humans in it, he enjoyed the prospects of dying. In all seriousness, he had wallowed for decades in the morose life. But part of him did not want to die. Part of him wanted to stage a comeback and build a reputation as an outstanding thinker.

Several years ago, forty to be exact, he came back from an acid trip where he had journeyed on the River Styx to the Valley of Doubt on an LSD trip and wound up seeking penance in Tampa for that excursion. It was there that he did time for what exactly amounted to as a transgression. The valley had rejected him, sending him hurdling on his way. The trek home had been arduous. A reincarnated soul now, no longer guilt-ridden, he must find Saw and try something else other than journeying in the past.

As he drove, his mind continued to wander. The thoughts continued to circle and circle faster. He had adopted Barabbas as an appellation, and it had been like finding an old long-lost friend. He visualized pigging out at the Last Supper and generally making an ass of himself on the cross. Choking on bread and wine, he was no better than a wino in a leper colony.

So, his suicidal ideation, his really wanting to die, was no more than scoffing now. Those young impressionable years have a way of drying out as a man gets older and quits drinking and drugs. Death comes nearer. Thank God for a second childhood. He had not been able to smile as a kid, standing before his parents in the family photos in a ghostly pose of a black and white figure in isolation. Thinking back to those days was saddening. Now that he was a kid again, why not smoke and have some fun?

Let Dr. Saw chop him to pieces. He would know if it was his time. Put his life in someone else's hands for a change. Relax, go with the flow, as it's been said. The big question was would some force or entity come down and whisper that it's not time. The rejection would be heart wrenching. He'd have to suffer a new complexion of aches and pains. It might appear to be a saving alternative to turn to the doctor, to get a fresh set of cells, to enjoy his vice with new impunity, but, again, the risks might outweigh the investment; obviously, a reason to not go ahead.

"Yes?"

"Dr. Saw, please."

"Do you have an appointment?"

Paul wordlessly produced the coupon.

"Come in."

The clandestine shack, if it could be called that, looked like a rubber room in a psych ward. The walls had padding. The operating table stood in the middle of the room. The nurse's desk was in one corner. Bionic arms, three of them, waved over the table like spiders. Laser guns and chest spreading claws with tweezer-like capability appeared, silently impressive. Quiet strength pervaded the stainless steel.

Paul stood riveted to the floor, his gaze going back to the table. Body parts he thought. "Go ahead, Doctor. Cut me up."

Anesthesia

Paul felt the injection from the needle. From there on in, it was all Dr. Saw. Saw moved skillfully, as though an angel in a cloud, cloaked in white gown, putting in a pair of specially made douche bags that were motorized to pump oxygen to every part of his body with osmosis sucking nipples on the outside of the bags. The bad lungs he tossed on the floor. Paul now had an operative piece of equipment that could handle the heaviest load of nicotine that he could possibly want.

"Wake up, Mr. Undres."

Paul's eyes slowly opened. He gave a wan nod. "I feel like breastfeeding."

"You are a pussy, Paul. And a coward. That was the mistake you made in birth. You opted to be a baby."

On top of being a cardiologist, a pulmonologist, a brain surgeon, and a psychiatrist, Dr. Saw was also an accredited counselor. He had more credentials than a purple heart recipient, but as far as public appreciation goes, Dr. Saw was an outlaw.

He had a fatherly view about him though. He smiled warmly at Paul as he sat behind Nurse Bite. A white Persian cat cuddled in his lap.

"Your chest is now hairless. The douche bags will last ten years. I examined your DNA and found the X factor. You are half man, half woman actually. Smoke as much as you like."

A blast of icy air hissed into the room and hit him in the face. He looked up at Saw, replying, "I don't get the connection."

"The man in you and the woman in you abhor smoking, but the rebellious child insists."

"You're kidding me!"

"I'm not, Paul. It's time you wake up to who you really are— a smoker in recluse."

His brow creased. "What do you mean, Saw?"

"You're an isolationist. But you're one of us, reluctantly, I might add A part, one small part, in the cog of machinery of man."

"It's communism!"

"The redistribution of goods can be handled by a computer, reliable and unbiased. Now all you have to do is have sex with the Y factor and spend your money before it is taken by the government."

"What else have you done to me? I don't feel right downstairs."

"I cut off your dick, but I put an airbag in your crotch to give you punching power. Your can have sex with whomever you please."

"You changed my sex?"

"Not exactly." Saw replied, pausing to make his point. "I reduced your manhood so you can flirt more evenly amongst the mob."

"Do you think reduced sex will get me out of my cigarette habit?"

"Listen, you are god's gift. In fact, you consider yourself so privileged that your life is not worth living, and sex is beneath you. Your seed has been wasted. You must learn to appreciate your seed. It is you. You must be thoughtful, generous and kind like a Boy Scout. Why push it? Because that's what dicks have done to you all your life."

"And I've been reconstructed by a nihilist! Dank you, Dr. Saw. Now, to fall in love."

The tone hardened instantly. "Love is for fools, fool. Wake up."

Getting Serious

What exactly did Doctor Saw mean when he said wake up? How awake could a man of sobriety be? He was seventy-one, belonging to the category of welfare recipients. He had consumed half a million in welfare benefits over the course of forty years. He had failed to grasp the simple edict of hard work. How else could he be judged?

A man has very few good friends. The mentally ill need no friends. They are held up by fantasy. Friends are irritants. A few are as adversarial as accommodating. He had worn out their indignation early on, but had made a lasting peace with them in the long run. Same with his parents. Nobody can be there for you always. That was what Bill Wilson had said. He would have to tough it out.

> *Let's start with me. I loved Paul in some fashion or another— either forcibly or regrettably. He never knew it. I've been in the background all these years. I tell you his story because I know him inside out. I'm his 'mother,' as he calls me. My thoughts are his thoughts. I've kept tabs on him all these years, waiting for him to simply say, "I love you." I'm ninety-one, and my years are getting short. I don't know if I'll ever hear that sweet sound from him, one expressing forgiveness. I'm only one voice. I go now, but hear me out. He must accept me.*

Was that him or her? He had trouble distinguishing his own mentality. Then, there is Matter, his telepathic chum from New York who taught him how to write. And Peter, another telepathic entity, who became his guide in a major trauma-inducing, overseas LSD safari. Finally, Brandy from high school, his only one true buddy who held no measuring stick over his head. Oh, let's not forget Toe, heavyweight of them all, who robbed and housed him at the same time.

Mix in Jell, his half-sister of the second marriage; Cason, his half-brother of the same lineage; Sunshine, his nephew; Cherry and Lonnie, half-sisters of the first marriage and voila, you have a competing mix that had finally resolved itself into a conglomerate mess.

Lung transplant or no, he was awake. He would not stay that way for long if he just sat around and did nothing. Even his smoke breaks could not break the monotony. He needed to step up and get out. He fought a wave of nausea.

The giddy tone of his life was about to change. He was involved with Chilli, hereto unmentioned, but a project of his because of his AA career. He tilted his head back and covered his face with his hands. Chilli! Christ, just thinking of her leaning on him constantly made him wince.

He decided to share with the doctor his latest concern about her. She had come as a dependent in her own right. Flaming red hair, a personality to match

, and a strike zone that included a bat, she had a highly combative moxie. What did they have in common? Crack, alcoholism, and schizophrenia. He recalled their first meeting.

"Hi, Paul." She offered him a clammy hand. "I remember you. Do you remember me?"

"I think so. You used me back in the day, right?"

"You gave me rides, if that's what you mean?"

"Do you need a ride now?"

A soft leaning forward, barely a whisper, and her reply. "That'd be nice."

"I can do that."

"You know, you're not as standoffish as you were five years ago."

He mustered a small smile. "I was a bit restrained, wasn't I?"

"What does that mean?"

"Hung up."

"For sure."

"Let's use each other then."

"I'm for it."

"What happened in those five years?"

"I was in prison."

Paul arched his eyebrows. "So, now you've arrested me with your winsome personality, hey?"

Chilli started laughing. Paul was so funny.

It had been another example of social accommodation. His thoughts drifted towards that so-called affair. She had become his friend; not his, hers. She was just a thing added to his plate of activities. She was not a person; she was a tragedy fit for a psychiatrist, a dope induced prostitute.

So, he was he was also a social being of twelve step work, the role assigned by Bill Wilson, cofounder of AA. Bill maintained it was the only way to overcome alcoholism— the tried and true method of maintaining abstinence, to help a fellow alcoholic. Of course, this was all Christian based horseshit.

Chilli, however, was far more than a simple alcoholic. She was a woman who made money with her pussy and smoked it up on crack. Unreformed as a devotee of respect. Yes, she had spent five years in prison. The rest of the time had been relapsing. He had been clean and sober for twelve years; she was relapsing every four days or so. Could he do for her what he had done for himself?

His approach was to get her into a rigorous daytime routine instead of sleeping from a frenetic night of crack. That meant accompanying him to his morning meeting followed by the gym.

Enthused about having a life, she had whispered to Paul one particular morning, "My boyfriend drinks himself into a noncompetitive state."

"Why don't you hit him like you do everybody else?"

"He needs twelve-step work, Paul. Can you help him too?"

Paul grunted. "You want me to save him too?"

"Yes, please, Paul."

"Sure."

He thought more about Chilli's accomplishments. She had wiggled her way into her boyfriend's clutches through a coincidence. Darin had had a roommate who had ordered a hooker, and she was it. She threw the roommate out and took over the reins of caretaking poor Darin. At least she now had a place to live. Her biggest fault was her bellicosity, taking umbrage at the slightest infraction. For example, Paul's advice.

"Chilli?"

"Fucking A?"

"Stop hitting people up. It hurts."

"I haven't touched you," she said.

"Dialogue is the closest thing I'm going to use on you. Let's try carrying on a simple discussion without a lot of invectives and manipulation of the car radio."

"Sure, bitch."

"I'm your bitch now," Paul had asked.

"Are you going to help Darin if I give you some?"

"Some what? Disease?"

Darin was hopelessly addicted to quarts of malt liquor and was stuck with her because he was too drunk to do anything else.

A DUI had eliminated her personal transportation. Darin didn't have a car, only a cane. Probation for her dictated community hours. It should have been reforming, but it was not. She was on pills, which were prescribed but nonetheless debilitating. Opioids to be exact. They affected her thinking, which basically consisted of sensation at any cost.

Paul had the car. His sole commitment to her welfare was to drive her around. No amount of talk meant anything.

"Dr. Saw, I'm serious about this chick."

Saw shifted in his seat, deadpan. "Seriously?"

"Seriously."

More on the Affair

To harp on her a little more. She was rough material. She had fought with the

LEOs, slang for law enforcement officers, for years. Assault with a purse, spitting, and kicking had resulted in felony charge after felony charge, meaning she had two, and one more would be the third strike and real jail time. That scared her.

But was that enough to abate her passion for crack? She was capable of more violence as long as her body held out. The body had outlasted the brain. While the spark was there, so were the pushers.

Pain pills and psych meds were only one link with reality. But they were the glue which held it together. As long as it was legal, it was appropriate. There were ostensible reasons: her back, her neck, her spine, and every vertebra. If she didn't have the meds, she would shrivel up in a worm like position and not move.

Drinking on top of them only added to the mix. She blacked out on alcohol and got blindly belligerent. At what point could he trust her?

"Chilli, tell me something about a sober life."

She fidgeted with a lock of hair, turning away. "There's not much to tell."

If Paul had said 'Why don't we talk about it,' she would have replied, 'Fuck you. Who are you?'

He wiped his palms on his shirt. "The whole thing boils down to getting your nut, doesn't it, Chilli?"

Her back straightened. "You drank. You used crack. What makes you so special?"

Paul propped his chin on his hand. "I've given it up for a new life. I'm clean now for the past twelve years. You know that."

A long silence passed between them.

She sensed his uneasiness and said, without turning to face him, "I'm trying."

Paul was at fault too. He had an attitude. Why not try sex with her after all those years of abstinence— and see if that works. Why not?

Look at him. He had driven her all over the county— to her pain management specialist in Oldsmar, Dade City for her shrink, and Brandon for her prescriptions. She was driven to get her act together; he smirked to himself. Paul didn't have his together. Why should she?

She sold herself. Everyone needs money. But survival was an afterthought. Cigarettes, clothes, fast foods were necessities. Her Medicaid check didn't go far. So, Paul was a special john.

And he did. It wasn't very climatic.

She liked the fact he didn't fall in love afterwards. But she wanted things, that was the catch. Since he was now part of her, it became a domestic chore. Regardless of issues like probation, DUI school, and court costs, she had a plan— take care of a roommate sloshed in beer, take her pills, and continue to take Paul for a ride.

The bottom line was she couldn't sleep or move without drugs, except to do tricks.

She had started in life young, lavishly making easy money as a stripper and club dancer. She still lived as if the pole was extended in her direction. But the axis was indisputably now tilted face down. She couldn't bear the truth that that life was over.

Paul could.

Her inability to think for herself frustrated Paul. She needed to be directed.

How did such a happy go lucky cyborg end up caring for a forty-three-year-old has been? Was this a post-operative repercussion?

"Chilli?" He asked, coughing softly then wiping the corners of his mouth.

"Yes?"

"Who's giving orders around here?"

"Neither of us. We're just small pieces." A small delighted smile came on her face.

"We're communists, hey? Just little cogs in the Big Gear."

"Try me," she said. "I'll gear you up."

"There's room for two bosses. I want you to boss you and I, boss me. That way, we have a semblance of knowing the direction we're going. going." He scratched his chin with a finger, asking, "What does illegality mean to you?"

"The cops."

"Inveterate drug usage and prostitution."

"Those are big words."

"Do you want me to explain them?"

"I do get into trouble when drinking, don't I?"

"Don't get rhetorical on me."

"I'm tired of your car," she said, tugging at her earlobe. "I need to get my driver's license back."

"You'll only get caught again." He felt a pang of frustration and exhaled slowly. He just couldn't plant the seed.

But a sterling lip piece at Atomic tattoo shop, a pair of butt tight jeans at Walmart, made her happy. "Let's shop and stop talking," she said.

"What else can you do?" he asked.

"Spread my legs."

Paul couldn't help himself. "Those fat things that expose a pussy meant for everybody?"

"Ohh…that hurts. I'm a girl, Paul. All of us have one. Does it scare you?

Mine speaks for itself. I have fun. It's that simple. Plus I get crack and that helps with the pain."

Later, when Chilli wasn't in the car, Paul talked to Dr. Saw on the phone. "Dr. Saw."

"Yes, Paul."

"I'm trying to help someone. As a trusted servant of AA," he answered.

"Really? Why?"

"I'm enabling, though."

"You have the money. You're a disabled vet. Wing it."

"Why can't I convince Chilli not to use? It would be so simple. We could goof off forever."

"She's corrupted."

"She's honest about it. That's one quality she does have."

"So what?"

Paul and Chilli had their moments. She was actually coming around. She had said as much.

The third of the month arrived. Her check. It was time to forget everything learned and get down. Waldo, a fawning idiot, who was in love with her, took her on a motorbike ride to Art, another welfare recipient. They partied like hell. When they ran out of money, she got belligerent with the wrong guy. Art leveled her. Bruised and battered, she took to the neighborhood's tented community near Waldo's Section 8 house. Feeling no pain, she wanted more bang for her money. Unfortunately, she had no more money. She sucked and sucked to no avail. In sheer mania, she called Darin, the roommate, and asked him to pay for a cab home.

That's the way the month began.

"The party wasn't all it was cranked up to be, Chilli?" Paul asked while in the car.

"I don't do crank." Her eyes widened.

His voice intensified as he continued, "The former Las Vegas girl who had been with the best is now the tattooed queen of the streets."

"Fuck you, Paul."

"Tell me about it. Walk me through it."

She stared at the window, saying nothing for a moment. Slowly closing her eyes, she breathed, "I don't remember anything except the punch in the face. It was a hell of a party."

The real party was just beginning. A curling up and hiding out until the next third.

"I am blameless, Chilli," Paul exonerated himself.

"It's your fault, Paul."

"Probably so."

I know you're trying to help me. I just get bored with life." The junior high dropout, the runaway, the dancing queen life of floating dollar bills, she didn't want to cross the line with him as she had with so many.

"We've already crossed the line, Chilli."

"At least you said 'we.'" She stole a quick glance at him. His jaw was set intently. The line was blurry. What was to be a romantic run of My Fair Lady was turning into a Dance with the Wolves.

She absentmindedly rubbed her nose with her left hand. "I respect what you are trying to do, Paul."

"Really?"

She pressed her hands to her cheeks, her lips parted slightly. "Making a woman out of me."

"You want me to propose, don't you?"

"I'd want to be your wife," she said, brushing a strain of her fiery red behind her ear. She placed a hand on his.

"You actually respect what I'm trying to do?"

"I do."

That was as dishonest as it got. He recalled a conversation with Dr. Saw.

"God does not give me more than I can handle, according to AA," Paul had said.

"He might give you less." A quick tap of the pen on the table was the doctor's opinion.

"I'm losing her."

"You never had her."

He pondered that as he drove.

The Roach

It boiled down to this. He could blow his own life by surrendering to someone using vodka, crack cocaine, and opioids. Not just her. It could happen with just one sampling for him. He respected that tenet of AA enough.

He went to AA for socialization. The strength of its membership was the overriding ethic not to use. He learned something in each meeting as he exercised his mind to the art of listening.

Another outlet was the computer, i.e., translate his issues into some kind of narrative that told his story such that there would be virtual witnesses to his problems. He had a cute way of paraphrasing to sell his ideas. His drive was to refine, polish his words to glistening crystallization, and add rhythm to his cadence, giving him some feel for consolation. A sentence that would tie the whole thing together made his day. Of course, the story was incomplete.

Chilli called, interrupting his ruminations. Her voice was pronounced. She told him that her pain pills and psychotropic pills were in need of replenishing.

Nobody just gets scripts of that kind without going through the hoops—even in Dade City where her psychiatrist worked. The psychiatrist was a friend. So, Paul and Chilli drove sixty miles to Dade City. After the shrink, there was the pain management specialist. That was in Oldsmar, another rural happening. Then, finally, the Brandon, where the only pharmacy that honored her heavy prescriptions existed. There had to be some sort of accountability for all the driving. It was the gas pump apparently.

Thought Paul enjoyed the pain management waiting room. The witnessing of souls who couldn't stand the slightest whisper of mental infraction was amusing.

The world went on its merry way during their excursions. One thing about Chilli was she had her prescriptions down pat. If only the rest of her life was similarly constructed.

There was a cast of other characters as well. Twelve-step work was limitless. The helping of slimy souls that permeated the woodwork was groundbreaking, the cockroaches that swarmed over him, overwhelming.

A creepy force drained him as he drained Uncle Sam.

Paul could use a good roach himself. Why not extend a little mania? See things in a different light with a brand-new perspective, hey? Get stoned.

The Four Roaches

But it was bug season. Crazy Crow, for example, was a good cockroach. He was a painter who fought the system who knew both Chilli and Paul. No one around was willing to sponsor a nature artist. He captured the look of life in a creature's eyes, whether it was the longing in an alligator or the reflexive gaze of a bird.

"Crazy?"

"Coo-coo."

The sound was vaguely reminiscent of a sound he had heard a long time ago. "Are you a bird brained today?"

"Coo-coo."

"Does that mean what can I do?"

"Caw."

"Tweet tweet, hello?"

"I'm in the crow's nest. I just saw big bird."

"Big bird? How big?"

"The bird of paradise. It just flew over just a few minutes ago."

"I thought you might need some straw for your nest."

"Like the matting for my paintings?"

"Yes. Chilli is indisposed. I need to spend some money."

"Help."

One word he had heard time and time again. "What do you need?"

"Some art supplies for the Lettuce Lake art school I'm starting."

"Are you getting paid for the effort?"

"Student tuition. I haven't figured out how much to charge though…"

Crazy Crow was having a hard time of it. He and his girl were being kicked out of their trailer. Apparently, he had finally come up with a workable scheme to make a little straw. But it seemed like the hard times just rolled on each other like a canvas stretched to the max.

Painting soothed Crazy's soul as writing did Paul's, but his girl's monthly check was not enough for them. Interference like car breakdowns, being kicked out of the trailer, mounting pressures that caused suicidal attempts by his girl were a weekly fare. Like Chilli, Crow had back problems too; but unlike Chilli, he didn't have Medicaid.

"When's the Lettuce Lake happening?"

"This month."

"A chance to finally do something constructive. A supplement to the check."

"I'm charging the kids twenty a piece, but the park won't allow it."

"How many kids will be in the art class?"

"One." The word was spoken with no fanfare, no shame. It was just the way it was.

Paul went ahead and paid for the brushes and the printing of his pictures at Kinko's. That was the last he heard of Crow.

Then, there was Waldo, already mentioned, the bike rider, who had departed from the normal crowd long ago. He knew a lot about fragmented thoughts. He worked as a CI, confidential informant, for the drug crowd and the legal crowd too, confusing the role so deeply that nobody knew whose side he was on.

He loved Chilli, but she spurned him. His check came on time too, and he spent it on Chilli's favorite dope in hopes of getting some. She was not stupid and gave him nothing. Diabetes was the one thing that curbed his appetite. He was almost epileptic. Between seizures, he called Paul.

"I gotta go to court."

"Another arraignment?"

"Yeah, the cops don't believe me." He gave a dramatic sigh.

"About what?"

"That I was not behind the wheel."

Paul took him to Plant City for one of his many hearings. Waldo had a pro se case against the charges. Several members of AA, Black Box Charlie for one, had tried to be an amateur attorney, thinking the rule of law was above the personalities who prevailed in the courtroom. Not in Judge Hack's domain, however. It had been a hard lesson for Charlie, who was now doing time, and Waldo was setting himself up for a similar experience. The judge ordered a competency test for Waldo.

He had only traffic fines to pay. The wisdom of paying the two hundred in fines as opposed to three thousand in court costs had no apparent importance. He was dealing with principles. It was his job to straighten out the prosecutor and the judge. After all, right is right and wrong, wrong.

A postponement was ordered after Waldo fired his public defender. A hearing was made for next month. They left the courthouse under the bemusement of the bailiffs and the smug satisfaction of Waldo. The latter was getting all the attention he needed.

A stint in jail had resulted in no insulin being available, and it had affected his brain. His desire to sue, on top of the traffic charges, added fuel to the proceedings. The little guy was of the conviction that he could win the big one.

The facts were these: Waldo was an odd ball whose brain had been damaged. Paul had to give grudging admiration to Waldo's insistence on defending himself and his apparent lack of fear of the courtroom.

Two slime balls down, Chilli came out of her coma. She was ready to listen. He picked her up with the expressed purpose of making a meeting. On the way over, she said, "Darin is such a loser."

He stared at her. "You browbeat the poor guy. He's a Zen Master of beer."

"You're the Zen Master, Paul. He is wasting away and wants it that way. I love him and want to protect him."

"From whom, you?" A soft chuckle.

"I get aggressive when someone threatens him, and I'm anxious for our future. He is using up his inheritance on my crack," she said, inspecting her nails cursorily.

"You crash in his bed in a flood of pills, intent to sleep it off and let whatever transpires in the dark to happen. Your mania upsets his Zen."

She held a finger to her lips. "I curled up in the garbage can last night. I thought I was a piece of trash."

"Garbage in, garbage out."

They arrived at the clubhouse. Paul went inside to address the congregates. Chilli stayed in the car. There is something about mornings. They offered a new outlook. He really wanted something to get something out of the meeting. Was he too naïve for Chilli? She needed backbone surgery. Coming outside to check on her, to see if she had driven off in his car, he spotted her on the patio. She was the queen of the porch. A broken back, a broken neck, her sagging butt line would never bring back the good ol' days but was no deterrent to the homeless hounds that lurked on the porch.

Inside was a period of calm.

"What is the topic?" asked Paul.

"Insanity," said the chair.

"That's crazy. Chilli and I were talking about that very thing."

"I said 'insanity,' not 'stupidity.'"

"Aren't they versions of the same thing?"

The meeting was over. Paul had his fix. He resumed his charitable role outside. Ordering her not to give any more money to the homeless, he directed her to the car. Tapping his fingers on the steering wheel, he asked, "Listen, Chilli, do you need anything? A cookie? A cracker?"

"Drop me off at Waldo's…"

He didn't want to get rid of her, but it was an opportunity. They made it to Waldo's. His house was full of junk. He watched them bicycled off. The exercise would be good for both. Paul knew they were peddling to tent city.

Three wry, rapscallion, tatterdemalion rogues— Chilli, Waldo, and Crow— had a common characteristic: a peculiar blind spot toward consequences.

Three clowns and the ringmaster himself, Paul. All in the circus of AA.

Once an alcoholic, always an alcoholic. Isn't that the saying?

Worn Out

He needed a break from the regrettable crowd. From abortions to Alzheimer's, the gamut of the untreated is a social fact. Leaving Chilli to her own devices was not going to work. He couldn't navigate her every mental twist, and he would not let her run him out of gas.

"Paul, they're trying to kill me." Her voice sounded familiar.

"Are they? Who, darling?"

"People! All of them."

He slapped a hand over his mouth. A fraction of a second later, he replied, "Invite them in. There's room."

"They are eating me alive."

"Offer them some crack."

Speaking of malfeasance, his family life had been conspicuously absent the last three months of his twelve-stepping saga. Cason had been fighting the good fight between his floundering law career and his care giving to the parents. He was devoted to Hymie and Nutty, who were at the nadir of their lives.

Paul needed to answer that call too. He had been voided of any compassion for them for so long that they seemed strangers. As a bachelor living life in solitude, he thought he might try a little reaching out to his loved ones, if he could stretch his arm. His presence, at least for an hour a week, might be a gesture in the right direction.

He and Cason needed no reminders of past failure. Both were in AA. Paul had an idea of exactly how much animosity the folks held for him, the same he had for them. The least he could do, however, is say 'goodbye.'

But his girlfriend first. Were people out to kill her? She was doing a good job of that herself. How many girls appreciated a supportive man? Not many.

How grand he was. There was no such thing as the untouched man he realized. He thought he might parlay Chilli as a buffer in a visit to his parents. That way, everyone could put her down and he would escape unscathed. Twelve years of sobriety, he was well rested now, ready for some good old fashion abuse.

He had fought hard to grow intellectually. The AA philosophy of acceptance and tolerance were tools of AA, but his insistence on ownership was his biggie. His goal was to die appreciated. Not before he kicked dirt on Nutty and Hymie, however.

He stifled a yawn. He would sleep on it. Without her or them.

Going Dutch

There was something very natural about prostitution. A person gets money for flesh. She admitted to violent proclivity, but to what lengths would she go to achieve crack induced godhead? Any available. She was absorbed by the foul acts which led to bliss. Life hadn't quite swallowed him up as yet. His seed was not for sale. No one wanted it.

"Look at me," she said. "Isn't it enough that I—I have a caved in chest, contusions on my head. I'm well aware of my mistakes. Isn't that enough?"

"Knowledge is painful, Chilli. Almost as bad as social repercussion. You may need more pills."

"Why are you so sarcastic?" she asked.

"Because you are a sarcasm. You've had a couple of beers, haven't you?"

"Yes."

The chemical change was obvious.

"It's the pain, Paul. I just want to kill the Goddamn pain." She drew in a long breath.

Paul was stumped. How does one overcome spasms of pain? Does one? "When you pick me up and take me for rides. Why do you do it?"

"You're the only friend I have truthfully."

"What do you want me to do?"

"Stop your profession, your business."

"You are my business."

He recalled what it took for God to eliminate his obsession to drink. On that last day at the VA, which was spent walking down a corridor, the thought came that the fizz of a Pepsi might be just as good as the bubbles of beer. That had opened a slight portal, and he drank soft drinks for a week. He hadn't touched another drop of alcohol since. It was almost as if it had been an experiment.

She, however, was a tougher case. She needed some insight too.

"They treat me like a subhuman, like an animal." Her shrill voice cut through the momentary silence that had hung between them.

"The 'they' people again."

She was serious, he assumed. "Listen, Chilli, you get pounded. No wonder you hurt."

She went on as though he never spoke. "Now they're trying to take my meds away."

"You can get more—" Before Paul could finish his sentence, she shouted, "There are no more."

Psychotropic medicine had helped Paul. But he didn't drink on top of it. As to their future, why not go Dutch? Wasn't that the nature of relationships nowadays? The problem with Chilli was she wasn't a partner, but an opponent. Her aspirations, if she aspired toward anything, was to be what Paul was, financially independent. The trouble was she couldn't get her way out. Nor could he. Going Dutch meant both parties could afford the joint effort. Chilli thought the idea absurd.

The concept of alcoholism being a physical allergy took the moral edge off being a drunk, but not a date. Paul didn't want a date. That's why going Dutch as a friend to a friend seemed so appealing. God is the champion, the ultimate breadwinner, let him pay. He is the Haver of an abundant life. People who follow his will are generally successful. Climate change, droughts and fires in the West, and snowstorms and hurricanes in the East are tests of His grace. Men must be willing to overcome any and all maladies. You can go kicking and screaming like Chilli or peacefully like Paul, but you will go.

Going Dutch meant little to the Beatles. The British Invasion introduced his generation to LSD. The world is so doped up now that it makes methadone just to taper off. There is no longer anything spiritual about drug use. Millennials are infatuated with opioids, meth, crack and heroin. The pill of the day is a prescription away. Very synthetic stuff. We have rehabs and halfway houses. Very dry music by pop standards. If Paul was to be an instrument of change, he had better tune up.

A Generic Folk Festival

Neither climate change nor overpopulation will prevent the greatest orgasm of all, the implosion of Earth, the upheaval of mountain and plain as the planet coughs up its belly. Those frequent and excessive happenings like forest fires, droughts, floods, and vicious snowstorms, which cost people everything they have, leaving them bereft of home and heirlooms in disaster after disaster, are more than merely worrisome. It's the geological zeitgeist.

The poor in Africa are sick and hungry. Bird flu haunts Asia. Before the crows eat the flesh, a faith that America will carry the day and save the world is largely hype. Between disasters, though, there is vaunted recovery.

The waters may never recede. Who will induce the moneyed to help out? Jesus, saint and savior, Mohammed, warrior and administrator, Buddha, stoic and sufferer, or Charles Schwab, stockbroker and money manager— who will guide the misguided? Which superhero will fly in? The belief that no matter how difficult life is, stealing is so much worse is pure capital.

His morality play was simplistic to be sure. Customarily, he and Chilli would kiss upon greetings, kiss upon farewells, but the tastelessness of their lives made even that repugnant. They were finished as lovers. She could have all the venereal diseases she wanted. She had danced for so many men for so long that, at times, all she could do was toss her hair and wiggle her ass. She was indeed the girl who had crossed the line and was now pickled and preserved. She awaited a fresh cucumber, but the boys were as pickled as her.

But the real folk festival was Mom and Dad. As he had previously ruminated, he would introduce her to family as a shield, someone to bounce off of. Maybe they would be amused and forget their bitterness.

The pleasant drive across the bay became tense when Chilli wanted a vodka tonic. She had him for a few moments. They managed to arrive alcohol free after passing bar after bar. Chilli's protest had been satisfied with the fizz of a Pepsi, no mere coincidence to his personal experience you'll recall.

Hymie, stepfather, loved her immediately. Here was someone solicitous, unlike his kids. He responded to her as if she was a sprite. Hymie told her silly jokes. Nutty was amused too. At her age, anything amused her. His mother's and stepfather's tittering resounded in the air and played like folk music to his ears. Paul shook his head; his mind floated away to a different conversation.

Cason, his half-brother, was the only skeptic. He confided to Paul that as a lawyer to alcoholics, he was of the mindset that Chilli would never make it unless she got off the patch and the pills.

That's how it stood. Mom and Dad liked Chilli; Cason didn't. The same could be said for him, except all three didn't like him. While it was a small folk festival, at least it wasn't raining like Woodstock. Nor was everyone stoned. Just demented.

Meet the Family

The scrutiny of his parents didn't stop with snappy remarks or one liners. Nutty, for example, loved books. She was quite the reader. Her offspring—none of them wanted—were compelled to put their angst to paper because of her deprecation of them. She would rather read than nurture. Going forward a generation, Cason's son, Sunshine, was a continuation of family scribes. He was an expressively powerful fledging. He not only wrote prose but wrote songs as well, posting them on the Internet.

Another artist in the family, Jell, Paul's half-sister, Cason's younger sibling, weighed three hundred pounds and hung out in Hollywood, California, selling celebrity clothing on eBay. She fancied herself a producer, a singer, and a playwright, and had some major accomplishments to show for it. Her words of choice were 'deprivation' and 'marginalization.' Her unloved self cried for food. What was it about the Eps clan that made all their children so hungry? The old man, who had been successful, personified the rule of thumb: the value of life was in dollars and cents which then made for unhappy merchants of humane sensitivity.

The thing about it was that all four— Sunshine, Jell, Cason, and Paul— were about to receive sizable inheritances. Hymie and Nutty were on the way out. None had reservations about the undeserved spoils. Each would get what they could. All were willing to fight for their piece of the pie.

And therein lay the puzzle. Would they spend more on probate lawyers than they would receive? Sunshine, Jell, and Paul could write all they wanted about being on about the stage on which they walked, but taking care of loose ends like their lives was secondary.

For example, Jell had, at one time, a goldmine on Forty-Third and Central in Manhattan. The lease for the subsidized apartment, which she sold for forty thousand, was now worth a million. She would have been set for life had she waited another year before moving to Hollywood. An asset like that would have made up for a lot of misery.

Cason, meanwhile, was laboring over no demand for his legal services and was simply resigned to taking care of Hymie and Nutty and the property as his job.

And the patriarch, Hymie Epps himself, stood resolutely sarcastic, being the only member who had been financially accomplished, whose claim to fortune was the two beach houses. He was now a crotchety old man with hearing aids. He considered himself the quipster, telling jokes no one wanted to hear.

It's nasty business, family finance. The three artistic autistics smiled. As artists, they might achieve stardom someday, perhaps going viral, but it would require marketing and that meant money.

They were unhappy at being poor.

So, they waited out Hymie and Nutty. Thankfully it wouldn't be long.

Swan Song

"Your family seems fucked up." Back in Tampa, Chilli said so.

"Yes, they are."

She stared straight ahead, blinking slowly, her lips a thin line. "I fit right in; don't you think?"

"I'm sorry I'm such a louse, Chilli, but we, we, uh… don't have any more room."

"All I do is complain. I want to be part of your loving family."

"You do more than complain. You fight uphill battles. When are you going to respect intelligence and persevere reasonableness?"

"What do you mean?"

"Exactly."

There weren't many ways to go for them. In the art of not making it, Sunshine, Jell, and Paul were minor actors compared to Chilli. She took center stage as in a comedy.

She loved, but no one loved her. He knew a thing or two about unloving natures. A cloud hung over him like perpetual mist in a woodsy Oregon township, and he was, perhaps, the most forlorn of all with the exception of Sunshine, who put mild depression to shame. Seeing himself as a protagonist in his book and seeing light under the tunnel as an antagonist, he would never win with those odds.

Paul Undres. He had been so undressed so many times, exposed for what he was, whether in the telepathic community of pot users or by jits in the hood, it was hard to be center stage with that kind of reputation.

And he and Chilli were at crossroads. They could either pull out separately or pull in together. She was still unattractive but smiling. Her back, her neck, her addiction to opioids and booze, and her small check was such that Paul's VA and SS would not be enough to buy her implants and pay for a spinal operation, as well as cover rehab, feed her, and buy her a car. He didn't give a shit about VD. If she hadn't caught VD yet, well maybe it didn't exist. He decided to play out the dance— even if it was a swan song.

It Gets Worse

What she needed was an actuary table complete with a life insurance policy, a little something for the future. She got Paul on the phone.

"Paul, this is Chilli."

"I know who you are. I'm resting." After a moment, he continued, "Okay, how are you doing? What do you want?"

"I'm practicing my dance routine." Her voice came out in slurs. "But I'm not feeling it."

"Who are you trying to seduce besides me?"

"I know you're afraid, and I don't blame you."

His words were as honest as his emotions. "I am afraid."

"You are the Zen Master. You have peace and quiet."

"I did."

"I need some mascara.""

He was amazed by the presumption. "Going somewhere?"

"Out," she said. Then, softly, "How 'bout you? Where are you going? To bed?"

"Hopefully."

"You're a bookworm."

"It still wiggles."

"But not for me, right?"

"It likes…" He paused for a millisecond. "It likes the soft earth, the dirt."

"I'm dirty."

"You have too many holes."

The conversation was going nowhere. He should have said it likes clean dirt. He could see her in his mind's eye. Her hand clutching the phone tightly, shifting her weight from one foot to the other. And, of course, a reflexive roll of eyes as she ignored all implications. "You don't comply with the law of human relationships. When you fuck, you fuck up."

"You're the only one who tells it like it is. That's why I like you. Everyone else likes what I have." She chuckled, but the sound was mirthless.

"How 'bout Darin, your roommate?"

"He's passed out."

"And Waldo? You two have been having some fun lately, haven't you?"

"I can't stand it when he kisses me."

"Have you finally given into him?"

"I haven't. I tease him,." she lied, matter of fact. "You're different though. I like you. You haven't fallen heads over heels in love with me."

"What's there to love?"

"Enough, Paul."

When he didn't say anything, she added, her voice singsong, "You cruise as though I don't exist."

"Let's go to a movie and watch some real characters. That's a good idea.. "

"I don't have the attention span. Buy me a vodka shot?"

"Drink some cigarettes, smoke some coffee. Stay with Darin and build a future."

"He's the ultimate Zen Master next to you. He's unable to feed himself, pisses on the floor, etc. He's not a real guru like you."

Paul rubbed his arm. "I've mastered the basics, yes."

Abruptly she said, "I care about my kid."

"I know you do."

"My mom means a lot to me."

"I know."

"I wish I could quit."

He gave a quiet acknowledgment.

"I'll be out on the street, soon, Paul."

"Walk the mile, Chilli."

"Listen, Paul. I get the distinct feeling you don't like me."

"You're wrong. I don't respect you."

War Buddies

Either go it alone or wait for her to grow up. He called her to see what latitude she was on. No answer. He knew what that meant. He needed a diversion, a break, a breather. He found it.

He had not been expecting it, but an old friend arose from the ashes of AA wasteland. Two years absent, he was dimly perceived in the darkness of the evening dusk.

It was Rufus. Back from a tour of Afghanistan for Critical Services, a mercenary outfit, he was out in the parking lot, 'decompensating,' as he put it, picking up cigarette butts, his version of twelfth-step work.

Sixteen months ago, when they first met, Rufus had impressed Paul with his combat dexterity by kicking with his booted foot the top lintel of the door leading from the coffee room to the main room floor, a feat that required full extension of a leg above his head. It was an accomplishment of wonder to Paul, whose legs were limited to stumbling.

Rufus had other talents. He was the quintessential liar, the prefabricator of tall tales. Paul was still at a stage where he believed what he heard. Why shouldn't he? He was a writer of fiction, but a soldier of truth. It was a constitutional requirement to his approach to AA.

A little history. Rufus had grown up in Denver, beaten mercilessly by a drunken father, and he had spent three years in reformatory because of running away sprees. He had wound up in San Diego under the auspices of a family whose son was Rufus' childhood friend. The friend had shared with his own parents the nature of Rufus' mistreatment, and they had taken Rufus in. A confused and bewildered young man, he skipped school in San Diego as he had done in Denver. He spent lots of time at the beach, and there, he was recruited by bikers to sell drugs. That worked out well for him. With every bust, the juvenile authorities bussed him back to Colorado to his generic family, where a gang member stood waiting at the depot to take him back to San Diego. "It was quite a game," Rufus had concluded.

Eventually, Rufus was court ordered to shape up. He had been caught too many times. He was to either enlist or spend time in the penitentiary. Special forces and Vietnam were his to have.

Now in the Club YANA parking lot, he had been deployed for the last time. His best lie to date was that he had earned a million and a half for his duty with Critical Services, which was due in his account by next week. His two children were both doing well, one an MIT professor, and the other, a Tampa paramedic. It seems prudent to mention that the man was childless.

There was no doubting his physical prowess or his lively, engaging style. Paul was entertained skeptically. It was a break from the dreariness of Chilli, but like her, Rufuse had no immediate money except the large sum awaiting in the mail.

What puzzled Paul was his gullibility. He was willing to be duped in exchange for entertainment. He was a willing participant in the game in exchange for buying hamburgers and cigarettes.

"Hey, man, long time, no see."

"Hey, Paul. Let's go get a hamburger. I'll ride shotgun. I'll tell you some stories." Rufus spoke fast and hard.

Paul bought him a Whopper.

"I need a place to stay tonight."

"Is that all?" Paul asked.

His rucksack became parked in the living room, Rufus began regaling him with stories. Tall tales of helicopters, wounded men, gun fights. It was \wide eyed fun— they went to bed at midnight. At 3AM, Rufus woke Paul up.

"I need a pack of smokes."

Nothing more needed be said. Rufus had rank. Paul wound up leaving his credit card at the store only to discover its absence in the morning at the all-night Starbucks. When he called the bank, three hundred was missing from his account. Another security leak, like the personages he hung with.

Rufus maintained he had a wife, a black woman who lived around the corner, but would not let him in. She supposedly held two jobs. They allegedly met in high school, but he had never gone to high school. Lo and behold, he had three degrees, the latest, a doctorate in medicine.

They went to Crystal River, Rufus' office in the woods, a double wide. Paul saw it, went inside, and verified its existence. That much was true.

Going back two years before this supposedly Afghanistan foray, his bill with Paul ran around two hundred. This time, he was only at two dollars and fifty cents for the hamburger and three for the cigarettes, plus the gas to get to Crystal River. The idea of being reimbursed with a piece of the million, perhaps a hundred times over, was actually pleasantly conceivable to Paul.

Rufus did one better. He promised a new computer and a letter from one of his higher ups that would qualify Paul as an eligible participant at the Tampa VA as a Peer Specialist, a job opportunity that had once risen but fast fallen.

"I'll call my Pentagon chief and see that he writes a letter immediately," he said, bobbing his head, up and down, rapidly.

"Go ahead," Paul shrugged.

Rufus proceeded to execute a call as Paul drove. "Robert, this is Sergeant Major Rufus. Good to talk to you. Listen… I got a man who needs a letter to the Tampa VA enabling him to volunteer. He's a good man. Can you swing that?

Was someone on the other line?

Why should Paul care? He had 100 percent. Maybe he could get 200 percent?

Nobody could do what Rufus did any better, lie with impunity. Two million for an extended tour in Afghanistan was not poppycock, but in that field of endeavor a real possibility that couldn't be discounted. And Rufus was unquestionably military. He wore camouflage clothing.

Paul thought nobody lied better except perhaps Elijah. Elijah was another vet who had been a roommate of Paul's years before Paul met Rufus or for that matter before he became clean twelve years ago..

Elijah claimed to be the ex-drummer for Marvin Gaye. Paul took him in wanting a roommate. They had met at an AA meeting even though both were still using. Paul was poorer then, in both pocket book and spirituality.

But the lies took an ominous turn once Elijah got the key to the pad. The mafia was after him. He needed cash to buy time. The ruse was convincing. Paul intimidated, gave him half his then 50 percent monthly allotment and did so for the two months Elijah ruled. Paul had initially liked Elijah, he grew to fear him. By the time Elijah was through, Paul's house was barely his own. Elijah finally left wearing Paul's best leather jacket.

So between Rufus and the memory of Elijah, Paul had had enough diversion. It was time to return to the safety of Chilli, the honest whore.

The Offer

Rufus left. Chilli was still around. She said she would never drink again; Paul knew it wasn't a matter of will. After all, he did have some background on that absurdity.

Whatever likeness it took, the truth was he wanted to undergo the scalpel again. Dr. Saw had been gravely mistaken about the air bag. It had no punch. He had thought about the virtues of being dickless. It had taken away all motivation. At least he still had his balls. Dr. Saw had not only fabricated a good story, but had taken drastic action. It had been more than a little fib.

Twelve years of AA had been devoted to this? Was he lying when he maintained he didn't mind. That was a lie. .He tried some honest thinking.

Dad, I love you. Hymie, I love you too.

Mom, you're the one.

Chilli, shut the fuck up.

Rufus, get lost.

Dr. Saw, restore my cock.

They were all lies. But the real truth was he was experiencing phantom feelings in the crotch. While it protected him from Chilli, it was disconcerting. If only he could save his manhood before it was too late. Maybe his dick was still lying on Saw's floor.

At last, funny, compelling Dr. Saw was back. Paul's lungs weren't the issue, his libido was. He remembered the doctor mentioning his prowess as a psychiatrist. Paul wanted to increase his libido. And he wanted his dick back. He'd have to have more than an airbag. He was not into crashing headlong into a relationship, but having something to barter with was important to a man..

"Saw?" Paul desperately wanted a meaningful conversation from the good doctor.

The familiar patronizing voice answered, "Yes, Paul."

"I never gave you permission to cut it off."

"What color do you want?"

"The usual albino without pimples on the head."

A soft chuckle. "Quite so."

"You better make it the same size it was. A little bigger actually."

"No problem."

The operation lasted ten minutes. The airbag remained for punch, but a twelve-inch appendage was added.

A rasped voice called out, "Wake up."

Paul looked down. It looked almost original, but bigger than life.

He went over to Darin's complex to sunbathe and swim in the community pool. With a towel draped over his head and basking in the sun, he was joined by Darin in an adjacent lounge chair. Chilli, ever-present, wiggled to the music from the radio. Paul closed his eyes.

She sneaked out of the pool area with the key leaving them both locked in. She finished a vodka bottle that Darin had bought for himself a few days earlier. He had drunk most of it, but there were still a few shots left.

She came back bubbly. The two remained sitting on the lounge chairs, their loins bulging. Darin was tanked. Paul was high on the cool water and the warm sunshine. She cranked up the radio and began her erotica. She thought she was making waves, but only nauseated her audience. She wiggled and rotated like she was a dancer at the Pink Lady. Engorged on vodka, she twisted and turned.

"That's it!" Paul stopped the charade. When they made it back to the condo, Chilli turned on the music channel of the TV set and continued performing.

"Gotta go," Paul said. He would save his dick for something less suggestive.

"Take me to a meeting." Her voice came out shrill. A single vein protruded on her forehead.

"A meeting?"

She tilted her head and smiled. "I need a white, pick me up chip."

"Why?"

"I drank Darin's vodka while you guys were sunbathing."

On the way, she said, "Stop up here at the Snax store."

"What now?" he asked.

She replied, wetting her lips. "I need to get a stem and brillo."

He winced. "No way."

She reached over and placed a hand on his arm, saying quietly, "Do it."

It must have been the next dick. He didn't want to use it. The final dance would be a touch of cocaine and then a john to pay for it.

Back at Darin's house, she got on the phone. "You deliver, right? I don't recognize your voice."

Paul merely stared; He knew this story well. At one point, he had a similar chapter. He fumbled for his keys in his pocket.

"You know me," the dealer said.

"I need forty."

The dope arrived shortly.

Chilli turned to Paul. "Want to stay?"

Sundays

His staying power was as short as his goodbye had been. Saturday was shot, and Sunday was not rich with possibilities either. The folks always came to mind. It might be time for some living amends.

His stepfather called him before he could reciprocate. On top of his suffering due to his immune system, the old man had insecurities about the future.

And why not? He had miscalculated his retirement income. He had never expected to live to ninety five. Being holed up in the beach house the last twenty years, all he and Nutty could do was drink to all their dead friends. It was called life expectancy.

Nutty had died last week, and he was now alone.

Paul learned secondhand his mom was missing. He saw her obituary. Nobody had told him.

Hymie's once a month trip to the cancer specialists at Moffitt was coming up Tuesday, and the old man needed a ride to and back.

"Paul?" The old man's voice was wavering.

"Yes sir?" Paul's voice resounded with concern. Was his stepfather actually feeling insecure?

"Just touching bases."

"I'm standing on home plate, Dad, not third, second, or first. I understand you have to be at Moffitt Tuesday."

"That is true."

"Cason tells me he can take you. After all, he attended Mom's funeral."

"You weren't there, I noticed."

"Couldn't make it."

"Why not?"

"Nobody told me."

"I guess we forgot." There was nothing apologetic about it. It wasn't seeking forgiveness or understanding. Neither was it expected. The point was it didn't matter.

"It's understandable," Paul responded. "About that ride, ask Cason… he's your real son."

"I can't hear you."

"You need to walk next door and ask him about a ride."

"I'll have to be there at seven o'clock and get out at ten. I hope they don't refrigerate me in the doctor's waiting room like last time. It gave me another cold. I couldn't breathe for days. Congestion, you know."

"You would think hospitals would be more considerate."

"Mercy."

"Mrsa, you mean."

"I can't take another cold."

"I'm picking up Chilli Tuesday for another round of recovery at Club YANA. Then, we're off to see her tattoo specialist, the one who gave her lip piercing last week. So, if I pick you up, you'll be blessed with her company. You needn't worry, her infections are of a different sort."

"I don't know if I can take it."

"Ask Cason for the ride then."

"I can't hear you. Repeat it slowly. You're slurring."

Paul grimaced. "You want a ride, Dad? Talk to Cason."

"I'll talk to Cason."

"You do that."

Cason, meanwhile, was butting his head against reality. He was optimizing new ways to get his name on search engines. His websites illustrated a basic flaw in his law practice; namely, he chose to focus on things rather than people. That's what happens if you're a lovelorn realist. He concentrated on the lowly flow of traffic violators rather than work for a prestigious firm, if there were any in Tampa. His specialty was drug arrests, but no one knew him. Thus, he had no clients.

Hymie called him in the middle of the night.

"Yes, Dad." A groggy voice answered.

"Paul will be busy with his lady friend Tuesday."

Cason fell back to his pillow and replied, "Don't worry, Dad. I got it covered."

"God bless you, son, for taking care of me. You will not be forgotten in the will."

Cason felt his stomach churn. Another unpleasant reality. "Let's not talk about it, okay?"

"How are the many cases you're dealing with, incidentally?"

"Let's not talk about that either."

"Paul has a new Prius… what are you driving?"

Cason replied sharply, "Let's not talk about it."

An impatient exhale could be heard on the line. "Jell has lost eighty pounds. How much do you weigh?"

"Fuck you, Dad."

Meanwhile, Paul was worried about his crotch. At least he had the original balls.

The Lay of Lies; Lie of Lays

Paul had weaseled out of the domestic chore. Back at the clubhouse, prevaricators were honing their skills. Dishonesty was running rampant in its course. AA was simply rife with cons. The role Paul took in the morning meetings was to enliven the group of deadbeats. It provided satisfaction that he could broadcast his message, that AA was a refuge for all alcoholics, including himself.

Yes, AA was a godsend. They offered a retreat from tiresome loneliness, self centered talk, and outlooks of a troubled mind. It was a place of calming comfort. There was a solid backdrop of support there, whether you liked it or not.

Paul was struck with the idea that there was the god of time and the god of space, both tightly interwoven. His gods were Hellenic, though the same battle on earth was taking place high above and beneath as well. His personal philosophy of the moment was that there were four gods: the *god of reason and the god of knowledge,* brothers in function, the *god of understanding and the god of doubt.* Four reasonably congruent lords.

There was nothing really to consider. They were out there and so what? It was a warm summer day. Spring had sprung. Summer was here again. Paul had his new lungs, his replaced crotch, and a new outlook. He took a deep breath. To the immediate god, it felt good to be alive, to start a fresh, new day.

Carefully, he spoke, "Welcome everyone to the Good Start meeting. I hope you all had a pleasant weekend and did not drink or use crack. My pigeon flew the coop. I have no one now."

After the meeting, Tony, an old acquaintance, approached. He spoke briefly and to the point. "Paul, how would you like a mail order bride?"

"I'd love one."

"Good, I have one."

"Let me have at her." .

"She's yours. I'll have her call you tomorrow. She's from Thailand. She spins like a top. Weighs ninety pounds. Black hair down to the ass."

Tony's words transported him. "Right up my alley."

"I came to this meeting specially to see you. I think you would be a perfect fit for her. I'm going up North, and she doesn't like the cold." Tony cocked his head and waited.

Paul slapped Tony on the back. "By all means."

Paul could easily abandon Chilli for a mail order bride. Did she have some vices too? He hoped so. Would he have enough space left to concentrate on his book? Who cared?

"She's thirty-one and tight as a mouse."

The call never materialized.

Nodding Out

Chilli was beautiful to look at certain angles and so vulnerable at times. How many times had he, too, crashed from crushing realities? For Paul, there was nothing to hide from anymore.

"Darin is Darin, Paul," she managed suddenly. "He bailed me out of jail. I smoked five thousand of his inheritance on crack. I owe him."

He jerked his head towards her, taking in her doleful eyes. "You'll never be able to pay that back."

"Fuck you," she hissed, suddenly becoming animated. "I'm going out to use. Let me out of this car."

Paul opened the door.

Higher-Ups

Was he too arrogant, too conceited? Is that what caused Chilli to refuse his help? The god of reason asked the god of knowledge for a clue what he might apply towards the god of understanding while the god of doubt smiled. The four lords chatted amicably overhead along with others.

The culture on this planet has gone to shit.

A subculture is the word.

How 'bout counterculture?

The hippies started the downfall.

The flower children?

And now we have AA.

A round of applause echoed, a faint drum roll could be heard.

They're legit.

Where did you hear that? From Mad Mothers?

They're not mad, they're heartbroken.

There has to be something positive in the world.

There is. Pessimism. It's a strong, vibrant force down there.

Man has a right to be discouraged.

How about the pensioners? They used to have a guaranteed income.

The discussion went nowhere, but it did open the door for the god of irony, a forgotten god on Paul's list. He only smiled.

The four exchanged looks, then asked the fifth,

> *How does Paul fit in?*
> *He's too smart to work. He's self-employed on welfare.*
> *He continued. He wants everyone to be supported by*
> *welfare. The affluent must be seduced into a gigantic pyramid scheme*
> *of assistance.*

> *There might be some percentage in that.*

The gods left it at that. However, the god of irony added.

The rich needed spiritual nourishing. The poor have

The last remark was a bit much, even for gods.

Zen

Chilli needed a fresh supply of scripts. Paul was able to dump her and deal with his own issues after half a day of trips to those by now famous rural happenings. On his own front, a VA CAT scan had proved negative. He was still healthy. His house was a tomb, however. The radio was silent. The magazines, unread. The place looked like shit. All the rubbish was on the floor. The roaches were sneaking in and out. His entire array of supplements cluttered the coffee table. Three rats had been recently killed in mousetraps.

It was time for a housecleaning. He kept the radio off but read his weekly collection of The New York Times, which had yet to fill the garbage can. Finally, he got off his ass and did his laundry. He swept up the floor. He made sure the dishes were stacked in the sink. The home was by no means spotless, but it was acceptable to his gaze.

He was the ultimate bachelor. He would not seek a job to satisfy the working public, nor would he buttress his fortress with an intruder. He had tried substitute teaching. He had tried enumeration with the Census Bureau. They both were suspect accomplishments. He remembered the old Assembly, Basic, COBOL, and Fortran days as a student when he had mastered the languages, but not the workplace. It was too late now.

He was virtually unemployable, the yardstick of compensation. The roadmap was laid out, spend that 100 percent. But how? He couldn't drink. He stared emptily at the four walls of his abode. Enlightenment would be nice. He went into a trance.

*Paul, step forth. Enjoy the riches that are yours. As
goddess of growing up, I remember you in high school
as someone who desperately wanted deep sadness
because it was easier to obtain than light joy. I saw
you disappear then reappear from the world of drugs
and darkness. Can you hear me?*

Paul heard.

*I remember you with the steely gaze, who could look
right into the marrow of a girl. There was the pure
Paul, the seeker of pulchritude. Somewhere, you lost it.
Whatever happened? It doesn't matter. You're doing
the right thing now. Continue to help people. You have
everything in place. All the dominoes are falling in place.*

Was this a true reflection? He hadn't even done his early morning routine of showering and shaving, and here he was hearing voices.

*The money you have now can be used in marketing
your book. Meanwhile, Chilli is a body of
impenetrable armor. If only she would give up and
surrender. How low does a girl have to go? If only
she'd learn that she didn't have to use and didn't have
to sell her body. She believes it's inevitable, that that is
her, and it is, but she's more. She must find it. No one
can stand the stress of the physical abuse she puts
herself through. Nobody can operate under the mindful
control of crack. Paul, either convert her or passes her
over. Darin will be hurt, but he's expendable. She loves you both.*

Paul said nothing, letting his mind absorb the thoughts

Give her time.

The house was still. He could only do what any thinking man could do, he called Chilli.

"I love all your imperfections," he spoke slowly, measuring his voice.

"I love you too," she told him. Her hand fiddled with her bracelet. "I just need…"

His grip on the phone tightened. "You need my attention. You will get up tomorrow."

"Yes, I will." Her voice sounded timid.

"Tomorrow, we'll begin a new life together. I'm taking you to get an MRI. I want you to undergo surgery. We will get you off the pain pills," he stated.

"I'm ready," she replied.

"Tomorrow."

The Machiavellian Slur

She just couldn't get up for tomorrow. It was too close. Ambien, the sleeping pill, the Latuda, the anti-psychotic, the Fentanyl, the pain patch, and Vicodin, the immediate pain relief pill, and finally, Zanix for anxiety— it was quite a cocktail. The Latuda, to quiet the thoughts, may have been metabolically friendly, who will ever know, but she drank on top of it. Moreover, not taking them as prescribed fouled things up too. It was really quite contradictory.

She was just too groggy to go anywhere. He wouldn't have an arm trophy for the morning meeting unless he felt like carrying her. He would have to experience the YANA crowd alone once again.

He decided to stay out on the porch after the meeting as was his usual protocol. He spoke with Scotty, whom he had benefited on numerous occasions over the years. From buying him a bike to a pack of smokes to five dollars gifts repeatedly, Scotty was perennial runner up for crackhead of the year— the past decade, really.

Paul was more engrossed, however, with discussing the state of the union with Jimmy, the black, who was the self-proclaimed non-racist of the group. Jimmy extensively promoted himself as the most misunderstood of AA people. It was to his self-satisfied ego , however, that he was put down by Paul for lack of education. It only made him speak with an accent.

Scotty diverted Paul's attention. "The mail order bride you bought into the other day was a bit Machiavellian of you, don't you think?"

"Machiavellian!" Paul exclaimed, delighted at the reference.

"You and Tony were treating the poor girl like property."

Paul crossed his arms over his chest, feigning a smile. "It's feudal to argue. I was being a prince of a guy."

"You can get a girl on Kennedy Boulevard for much less."

"That's your turf," Paul replied. "Maybe it's the reason you have HIV."

"That's licentious, Machiavelli!"

"What are you, some sort of wordsmith now? Has the crack given you insights into useless references? Having you been hiding out at the library?"

"Using money behind a girl's back is an act of a dictator." Scotty continued.

"Here's a fresh pack of cigarettes. You didn't even have to ask. My acquisition of Tony's wife was pure protean."

"What the hell does that mean?"

"I didn't think you know. Her acquisition would have shown my flexibility as a man. I'm that fluid, Scotty."

"Your theory leaks. Just because your welfare check is larger than mine doesn't imply you have anything over me or, for that matter, can buy me off with a pack of cigarettes," he replied.

"You're not the prize I'm after. She is. A commodity has some value, Scotty."

"Where's Chilli, by the way?" Scotty asked, changing the subject.

"Chilli has purchased a new man. She has changed me. I'm involved in the human race again. She has taught me several things, namely, the worth of keeping clean. I've awakened to new excitement. Dr. Saw saw to that. Tony, meanwhile, offered unimaginable heights but no product. It was all his imagination."

"So?"

"I have Chilli. Many jerks have no one," he said, then quickly added with a dismissive wave of his hand, "…you included."

"You could have been pampered by Tony's woman. You wouldn't have to buy his wife anything. I suggest you take her, Machiavelli."

"I tried."

"Become the ruthless dictator of Club YANA. Own every girl at Turning Point. It'll cost, but it'd be worth it. It's the principle of chauvinistic priorities."

Paul's slapped his thighs. "A Boccaccio tale in modern times."

"By the way… I haven't eaten in days."

"Good for you, you're on a diet. Even though I owe my swag to Chilli, I'll buy you off."

"Every time I get high on crack, I get a woman," Scotty added without regard for the impending gift.

"Try saving some money for a bus ticket. Seriously, do you need a lift? A bite to eat? Name it, Scotty. You've earned it."

"Five."

"And what about me taking over Tony's prize possession?"

"Caesar rules, Brutus."

"She was Cleopatra in disguise. Here's five. Don't pay me back."

Scotty raised one eyebrow. "I won't."

Paul left for the gym. He had gotten off cheaply once again.

On Again, Off Again

Yes, Chilli had given him swag. Surely, she had a sexual transmitted disease, if not several. It might take more than money to straighten this out.

The old adage goes… history repeats itself. She couldn't make it the next morning either.

"Chilli?" he had called.

"Yeah?"

"I need to be straightened out," he said, drumming his fingers on the wall.

"I thought you didn't want sex with me?" She said straight up.

"I don't, but I want you up. Are you going to get up?"

"I'm not going to charge. It'll be a freebie."

"I'd be eternally grateful if you could just get it up."

"I don't encourage that sort of thing. But I love you for what you are trying to do. You actually care."

"Yes."

There was a long silence.

"Take your meds and go back to bed then."

Chilli shook her head, dispersing a thousand cobwebs. "There are tricks to be had. I have to make some money. But my back is killing me."

"It's Wednesday. Hump day."

"My special time of year."

"You can go to sleep now, wake up in the middle of the night and be manic until dawn."

"That's the way it is."

Her words penetrated his mind. His assessment was that Darin was passed out. Waldo was home kissing her image. Paul realized she would not give up trying to make it financially the only way she knew how. Men to her were worth no more than a plug nickel— to put it musically— a C note. She took her thirty pills and returned to lala land.

Three days later, Paul got through again. "Where have you been?"

"I'm not sure," she answered, rubbing her eyes with the back of her hand.

"You have had seventy-four hours of nightmarish internalization. Why not have some fun for a change."

She shook her head. "It's very fulfilling, nightmares. They satisfy a subliminal instinct. I'm quoting you. I could never use those words myself."

A distinct sound could be heard from her end of the line— a chair scraping the floor as she dragged it to her and sat down. "Has it been that long?"

"It has."

"I can't take it," she whimpered.

"You have to."

"Don't let me do it, Paul."

The melodramatics of the call did not escape him. He understood her twisted propensity. "I can't stop you until you find a different god."

"I don't want to…"

"You have to."

He picked her up. They drove to Club YANA. Her doses of medication meant no pain, but whimpering and whining were still in. He had years of experience on Thorazine, Melleril, and Lithium. They were barbaric and invasive, the infancy of psychiatric medicine. The medication he took now wasn't nearly as detrimental and a thousand times more effective. Had he paid the price with those hard times? Was there a latent credit to that suffering? Would she have to suffer forty years like he did in order to have a psychic change of equal equivalency?

Do the Math

The argument that the helping of suffering alcoholics would ensure his own sobriety bothered him. A stark staring at who he was in terms of his history was sobering enough. The AA triangle of service, sobriety, and unity wasn't entirely congruent in his eyes. A haphazard trapezoid was the geometric puzzle he found himself following. What angle would he employ to get a proper measurement of things? After all, that was the essential question. The Geometric Expert, the Theorist Behind All Complexities, the Axiomizer of All Axioms, and finally, the Proof Reader of Personal Stories was silent on the matter. Figure it out yourself was the mandate.

She finally got out of bed. She could walk! He took her grocery shopping. They went happily up and down the aisles. He followed her every move. She was in her element, buying. Her fierce glances at the food products, her deliberate throwing of the stuff into the basket… it was truly fascinating. He slipped off to a separate aisle and made a call.

"Saw?"

"Yes, Paul?"

"Of all the body parts you reassembled, did you ever have one that was a brand name?”

“Why would you ask such a preposterous question? I thought you were in recovery with emphasis on the here and now?”

“We’re buying products untested here at the supermarket. Just because you ruined a perfectly good body, doesn’t mean I’m not curious as to the validity of shopping around.”

“You’re asking about Chilli, aren’t you?”

“She’s throwing everything into the shopping cart. Yes, I am.”

“She is a basket case. Toss her to the butcher.”

“I don’t want her cut up like so much meat. I just want to know how to freeze this moment.”

“Come on in,” Dr. Saw countered. “I’ll fix you up.”

“Hands off, Saw.”

“I live for my patients.”

“Just tell me, since you are the most amoral man I know, is there hope for her?”

Dr. Saw paused for a brief moment. “Let me operate on her.”

“I’ll think about it. Do I need another coupon.”

“You’re a supermarket. They have plenty. The rewards will follow. How are the lungs by the way?”

“I went in for a CAT scan at the VA. I think the suckers on the douche bag are clogged. Chilli tells me my breath smells like plastic.”

“She smells too, doesn’t she?”

“She has food stamps.”

His face broke into a wide mile grin. “Excellent. Bring me a sandwich.”

High Heavens

It looks like Chilli is subverting our realm. Paul is getting in deeper and deeper. He's suckered the god of water with his protean bullshit. He's trying to operate with the surgical precision of Dr. Saw. He's uncovered the god of math, the number cruncher, the chief operator of mischief on this planet with Chilli's food stamps.

He'll never crunch the numbers. That god is a source of irritation for even us.

The remaining gods shared a good laugh, eyeing each other with undisguised suspicion.

Let's fill his douche bags.

Paul's the most dedicated twelve stepper we have. His only insistence is that the Big Book be rewritten. That's a big task.

Chilli is a source for dying men like him. He might go before her.

He doesn't have that much time left. She won't last long after either.

No one else gives him what Chilli does.

Which is?

A migraine. It's a no-brainer.

If he wants to join us, he's going to have to put in the effort.

Their voices echoed through planes of time and space. Everyone grovels to get here.

They're both worms. They deserved to be planted in dirt. That qualifies them both.

As what?

It was a question the gods of doubt had posed. The gods of second guessing laughed. *Entrants to the heavens, of course.* The hysterical gods of history then spoke.

> *Chilli's faults are obvious. Remember, however, Paul*
> *got clean in the VA hospital, where the fizz of a Pepsi*
> *was just as good as the bubbles of beer on the day of*
> *9/11. And after that, he was imprisoned for underaged*
> *sex of which he was later released. Now he's simply*
> *trying to regain his manhood as a human being.*
> *And he wishes to stop smoking. Outrageous.*

A Satisfying Concept of Self

The gods above and the gods below, of which we've heard nothing, and the people in between were feverishly trying to formulate some kind of relationship with Paul. But Paul wasn't buying it. He was the sole filter through which he saw things. A man has outer power and an inner power. Both are separate in one sense yet connected in another. It is the responsibility of the inner power to perceive and to coordinate with the outer power and make things happen.

Hell was calling. Not everybody wants to go. The heavens. for there were many, was standoffish. Cliquish, you might say. Whether it is atop Mount Olympus or just a cloud set up by a device driven memory bank, they were largely theoretical.

Dr. Saw was the ultimate curator of the earth bound. He was a labor-intensive fool who was no more concerned about his work than his art. But he made life on earth operative.

Life is a moral trap. Everyone steps on it. Chilli did it like it was her natural gait. As for Paul, old derelict chums protruded. Realistically, he smoothed over them with deliberation. If only his peers would stop peering.

Why relive the past? Because it was the backbone of his experience. At one time, he had it all, but lost it to the Berber in Morocco. Why not become god centered again? Because he would be fucked again. Yet mental acuity is the result of the inner power. Acuity requires precepts, adaptations made in the face of adversity. Letting it all hang out is a sign of weakness, yet we all do it on occasion. Productive work is the execution of a personal plan. He was working; he was writing.

Could he get in a few quick years of satisfaction from her before she broke down completely? Could she be of service without his dying in the attempt?

And how 'bout his nuclear family? They were all slow learners. Hymie, Nutty, Cason, Sunshine, Snotty, his real brother in California, and Jell, and Paul too. No matter how dumb, Paul was prepared to give Hymie a portion of his 'allowance' to use in his retirement. He didn't want Hymie to spend his last days in total bitterness. .

So, who was the monetary god in the family? Jell? She had managed a flow of handouts from Hymie for years. Cason? He was working his ass off caretaking both Dad and property. If ever there was a need for a lawyer, it was as executor of the estate, separating the various egos, conflict of interest not-withstanding.

So what was wrong in the past deserved burial. Unhappy youngster, hip-pie, flower child, pot head, acid freak, Airman, medicated vet, and now, twelve stepper, Paul had a long history of wrongs. But he had twelve years of rights too. While he had outfoxed society's toughest accountants, the bottom line was that he was emotionally broke. And thus, he approached his mentor for answers.

"Saw?"

"Yes, Paul?"

"What do you think of the pure Zen state?"

"I'm a communist, not a Buddhist. I believe in state owned property. That's why I transformed you. I get a big kick out of fucking capitalist pigs."

"I'm hardly a capitalist, Saw."

"You're an American, and that's good enough."

"You live here, for Christ's sake!"

"I'm subversive. Okay?"

"I need an ally."

"You have three: your so-called book, Chilli Peppers, and your family. They all weigh on you. Ignore two out of three and publish yourself.

"I don't want to be famous."

"You're anonymous now. How does that feel?"

"You're a mortician, not a doctor of healing," Paul said.

"What do you ugly Americans know?"

"We rebuilt the world."

"Like the twin towers of high finance?" His tone hardened as he added, "Dasvidanya, Paul."

The Beautiful People

So, he had no class. The beautiful people nauseated him. He was too ugly. No degree of comradery could be found with the beautiful people unless he got published. They were out there— holders of beauty, themselves porcelain portraits of TV and magazine. But they were fragile too. Everyone had their Dr. Saw.

Paul's identity was mired in the faceless crowd. He was beautiful inside. That was questionable. Each scathing glance from a shopper at Walmart bespoke something else, else why the looks of scorn? The identity of the black man, the identity of the veteran, the identity of the workaholic, the identity of women, and the identities of dogs and cats, it was creepy.

But what of the beautiful people? They were objects of affection by movie goers. They were the gods and goddesses. The conversant, the glib. their smiles radiated fresh teeth, if not arrogance. Maybe he should pander to them and forget the AA crowd.

But even the beautiful people are susceptible to alcohol. They usually wind up in the most resplendent of rehabs.

He hated movies. They were so obvious.

He made a meeting. He started with his usual, "Hi. I'm Paul, and I'm an alcoholic."

"Hi, Paul." The chorus of voices reverberated.

"I'm tired of spending my resources on cigarettes. I want to lead a beautiful life."

"You are the smartest of us all, Paul. Your books make people laugh. You're a celebrity."

"The Step Series," he boasted. "I tell AA as it is, don't I?"

"People are dying to know the final chapter of Paul Undres."

"He's cold hearted and mean, but not out of touch." Paul said simply. Then he added, "We all go, rich or poor, to AA for decades, day after day, month after month, year after year."

"The plan is to survive, is it?" one member offered.

"Give us your plan, Paul," asked another.

"To be an indie author and avoid the traditions." Paul gave his best smile. They were yellow.

Dad

His stepfather cut him his quarterly inheritance check from his real father's estate, which consisted of an interest-bearing account for Paul. The other children, kids at heart, had received one hundred thousand in cash, but Paul, because he had been a crackhead, was denied the principle and got only the interest. That was totally unprincipled he felt.

Not only that, but his house was in the ghetto, and the neighborhood knew him well. His identity, immersed by unfortunate experiences with crack dealers, was tightly wrapped. He had fucked up, and as in his father's case, was paying for it.

Fruits, his stepbrother on his real dad's side, was in charge of dispensing the interest which he did to Hymie for Paul's benefit every three months, leaving Paul completely out the transaction, only denigrating him further.

"This is for you, Paul," Hymie said.

"It's not much, is it, Dad?"

"Why must we be so mercenary? If I hadn't told your stepbrother of a wiser investment than a mere savings account, your interest wouldn't be nearly as sizable as it is."

"Yes, I do owe you, then."

Hymie's eyes barely concealed a glint of utter disdain. "You're going to owe me a lot more when I die. I am approaching that time in life when the benefits of my hard work are going to go to your fruition. What good it does, I can't say. You never listened anyway."

The phone rang. It was Chilli. "Paul?"

"I'm busy talking to my stepfather."

She sensed money. She knew perfectly well the tenuous relationship he had with his stepfather. "I don't have to go to church today with my mom. Do you

"You're on the speaker phone, Chilli." He turned to stepfather, scratching his head. "Ignore her, Dad… she's being metaphorical. Not now, honey."

"How much is your father giving you?"

"More than enough."

"I'll go to the bank with you if you want."

"What can I do for you, Chilli?"

"Oh, nothing."

He disconnected. "Turn off the TV, Dad. I want to talk."

"I have nothing more to say, son."

The inheritance check mattered. It paid the three hundred a month drag the cigarettes were costing. But what else was it costing? A day spent with Hymie was a day in bitter reminders. Actually, he preferred scorn to understanding.

"Here's some food for you. It's a half-chewed steak and half-eaten baked potato."

"I'm not hungry."

Death Day

So, Hymie was dying. Mother was dead. It was the middle of May, hot and sweltering. Paul was celebrating another anniversary in sobriety. He had been clean now for thirteen years. Mother's Day had come. Next month would be Father's Day. Then, the next month would be Independence Day. Sandwiched in between was Memorial Day, celebrations of soldiers who had made the ultimate sacrifice.

How about a day devoted to death in general? Death Day, a celebration of no more? To fully recognize death as part of life. None of its weightier aspects

— like regret, loss of loved ones, funerals, etc., but the joy of exit.

The nihilism of the new century calls for at least one day devoted to dying, which come to think of it, will be parceled out by God in each and every case, no matter how strong the disagreement or what day of the year.

The world is animated by droll interpretation. Computer graphics rule relentlessly. The Simpsons have taken the place of such stalwarts as Jackie Gleason and Ed Sullivan. People suffer through eye-numbing screen art.

Onward and upward, as they say. As a citizen of civilization, death is the way out. Welcome it. Acknowledge it. Make it a part of your plan. Life is part time, no benefits. Death is permanent. When life is not good, death is. When life is, death is not. They're polar opposites. How many dimensions are there in death? Zero.

Paul celebrated his sobriety date at an AA meeting, putting death day on the back burner. He did it alone, without Chilli. He made no speeches. He had made a point of saying nothing. He knew the gods appreciated a man of few words.

Heavenly Chatter

So…Paul wants Death Day as the official day of reckoning.

He wants to break from the moneyed crowd…and be beautiful inside." A silence fell upon the group.

He thinks being boss is boss. A CEO by proxy. What's his business plan?

To get by.

The economy sucks.

That's popular opinion.

Hard work doesn't pay off. There's no middle class.

They were classless to begin with.

*If everyone becomes highbrow, then who will do the
dirty work?*

The youth.

They serve in the military.

The immigrants

The government only allows people from Norway now.

The Mexicans.

Bueno.

He smokes still.

He's willing to face the consequences, at least before they happen.

He has his death day picked out.

He's never been really sick.

*Mentally, he's mature. I think it's time we induce a little
compassion in him.*

*He must own up. He simply can't continue to exist as a
cavalier welfare recipient and an authoritative figure
of literature both.*
When we reconvene… let's hope he has quit smoking.

At least he's leaving something behind.

What?

Cigarette butts.

The Real Red Read Herring

The gods were all over themselves, spilling the beans. Maybe their thoughts would combine with a little effort from Paul and produce an authentic text, a read herring of red herrings, namely, an entire book as to false clues for the living.

What a misleading idea! There are many reasons for life, but it all started with one. No red herring could possibly misrepresent that. But the thought that began the universe, as inanimate as it was, had long since been left behind, replaced by animate beings who had thoughts of their own. If life was meant to recapture, uncover, relive that magic moment, or simply to be in touch, it was beatific at best. It was catch me if you can at the speed of light. Yet life was coming to a close. At least this spin cycle.

Babies cry because they're upset. Men kill each other because they're angry or greedy. Women deny sex. All because of an infinite universe which leads to such confusion.

The thought as a leap of faith requires risk. No secure, confident person would pray unless there were some valid reason to do so. Who else is there to turn to other than one's imagination? Fortunately the world of ideas circulate, becoming answerable in due time. Think large, be large. For Paul it meant go for it.

So he knelt next to his morning coffee cup and pack of cigarettes. His leap was the old familiar rendition of time and space, a vocalization to an abstraction, deceased parents perhaps, no one else in particular except an empty god. It brought him back to earth. He had no out of body experience. In fact, his prayer, his leap, had been nothing more than a wish not to jump to conclusions.

He remained faithful, however, uttering these words: "Gods, if you can hear me, forgive me of my habit. I want to live."

Paul was beginning to think all these prosthetics of Dr. Saw were mechanical monsters. Maybe it was the gods' plan to allow Paul his little habit. Smoking is just a disease like life. Why not enjoy the mother earth's tobacco and be planted later?

The red herring of all this was his nerves. They made him nervous.

Ping Pong and Golf

Life up to now had been like a ping-pong game, following the logic of the bouncing ball as it went back and forth over the net. Instead of chasing the ball, whack the damn thing back. It is no better to come up with a weak conviction and sink the ball into the net than a strong conviction and overshoot the table. The point is lost anyway.

Remember this: The stylistic player collapses the ball into the net and loses the game because the more physical and less graceful opponent plays the person rather than the ball. So, forget style, get physical. No matter how many artful slams, the showboat eventually catches the net and thus the game.

He wanted to go to Dr. Saw for another MRI. He needed a full X-ray to find out how much longer he had. .

He was not a fatalist. He was not a pessimist. He was both. Even though he would die completely and fully cancerous, he wanted to at least tackle the cancer problem at its early stage.

Now this— fifty years of tobacco filled all the holes left on the course. The greens were brown; the water holes were steeped with golf balls. But they were his balls, his life.

He had striven to be the smartest tobacco user on the planet. He was sure he did not have much competition.

Mary

Chilli was a child he could easily understand. Unlike Darin, Paul simply directed her. Due to certain parameters, he would not get involved any more than he was— restraint was his byword. Therein lay the question. How could he love a woman who was obviously a piece of shit? It was simple: he was shit too. But he took laxatives, while she was stopped up. It was all so simple, he thought. While he didn't love her intellect or her body, he allowed her to love him. Thus he would be dragged down. Perhaps his pernicious cigarette habit was the cause. He knew he was going to die soon. Of course, the bottom line was the friction between the two. Well, there you have it. Abrasive behavior.

Adorable children are loved all the time. Chilli was adorable because she looked up to Paul and worshipped him although you would never know it. He didn't really care to be Zen Master and rule an empty head. His new set of lungs was expelling gusts of energy he didn't know what to do with.

Meanwhile, his appetite for cigarettes was growing larger than his legendary appendage.

He decided to go to his high school's fiftieth reunion. Perhaps it would provide some answers. Up front, he forgave all his classmates for their disrespect. He intended to read a chapter or two from one of his books. It would be the first time he had ever talked to any of them. He would drink his black coffee and stand out at the cash bar with his dark beverage while his classmates got rip roaring drunk. He would pay the price of old memories with a standup performance.

He thus attended the affair at the Hilton.

"You remember me, Paul?"

Paul looked up and gave the man a small smile. "No."

The man struck up a conversation that had no prelude of any sort. "Mary had to have an abortion, you know."

"Mary who?" Paul replied. "Oh yeah, Mary."

The man took the remark in a stride. "It's a scar that has never healed." His voice shook with pain.

"Where is she now?"

"Dead," the man answered, his gaze boring a hole into Paul.

Paul didn't speak and merely nodded, somberly. After the man left, Paul decided to go home. His thoughts flowed, uncontrollably not his.

> *I'm your first lay, Paul, the one you were incapable of*
>
> *loving. I'm one of the goddesses now, not your mother,*
>
> *but I do have her permission to speak. I carried your*
>
> *kid until the abortion. I remain scarred to this day and*
>
> *no longer love you. You will never bear children*
>
> *because of my scar. I'm Mary of section 6, Wilson*
>
> *Junior High, and I now await your arrival in order to*
>
> *shower you with my loathing. The thought monster*
>
> *rumbles here, and I'm going to add to the uproar.*

Paul sat in the chair, spellbound. Mary, yes, Mary. He vigorously shook his head. The ownership of this particular vendetta wasn't his, but hers. Would he actually have to put up with Mary's bemoaning in perpetuity?

Yes, he remembered Mary. Who could forget? She was the only girl who liked him back then. Another case of premature, consequential penile pursuits. At least, Chilli couldn't get pregnant, he thought.

The Timer of the Gods

> *You never told us about your kid, Mary.*
>
> *He didn't know. I dropped out of school.*

There was a quietness to the voice, a calm settled assurance to it.

> *You married a dentist,*
>
> *I can smile about it now.*
>
> *Who cares?*
>
> *You sound like Paul.*

There was a moment's pause before Mary spoke.

> *If Paul can turn his life around, I'll forgive him.*
>
> *He lives in a country that supports him, but not enough money to support a kid.*
>
> *Political activism is the only hope for Paul.*
>
> *He'll never enter politics.*
>
> *His mind is a fucking partisan gridlock of himself.*
>
> *He is truly manic about himself.*
>
> *Thirteen years of recovery have been devoted to liberating him from psychic capture. Let him simple die of a stroke—*

It was as though something had been revealed to them in glorious pristine clarity. They spoke in unison,

> *He must salvage Chilli and himself. He must quit smoking as an act of common sense.*
>
> *He is a pack of lies with a pack of cigarettes.*
>
> *Time will catch up to his dishonesty.*

Tick tock started the clock of the watchful.

The Chamber of Commerce

Contrary to popular opinion, Paul did get into politics. He had a real plan. He decided he would make a contribution to society— in the form of urban planning. He would become a health consultant for the Cigar City, Little Havana, i.e., Tampa, Florida. He would make it the first smoke free city on the East coast.

Wisps of the movement were underway in California, but to become a smoke-free city on the East coast was a dying need.

"Is this the Chamber of Commerce?"

"Yes, sir…it is. May I help you?"

"You may."

"Yes?"

"I wish to speak before the chamber at their next session," Paul said, his voice deliberate.

"We do have a guest speaker format. Let me transfer you to the presiding president."

"Go ahead."

"Hello? To whom am I speaking?" Paul asked.

"Mr. Nuccio."

"Mr. Nuccio, I wish to address the chamber in short order."

"What is to be your message?"

"I want to make Tampa a smoke-free city."

"No cigars, Mr. Undres?"

"No cigars."

"I'm afraid that's impossible."

"Nice talking to you."

"On second thought, we want you to air your ideas."

Paul held the phone tighter, "My stepfather was once president of your organization."

"What was his name?"

"Hymie Eps."

"Oh, yes." The man croaked. "And you are his son?"

"Stepson."

"Do you have a methodology for enforcing a ban?"

Paul smiled confidently. "Arrests, just like a DUI charge. Reckless smoking."

"It would be contested legally," Mr. Nuccio protested. "We can't afford that."

"Smoking is bad for your health," Paul stated categorically.

"It's the legal fees the Chamber is concerned about."

Surreal wisps of memory floated into his consciousness. "Nothing in a sober society changes unless you challenge precedence. It's time to legislate a law against smoking."

Mr. Nuccio hesitated. "Mr. Undres, we want peaceful change."

"I want to light a fire in Tampa town, Mr. Nuccio."

"I'm a heavy smoker," Mr. Nuccio leaned forward as he replied. "You got the wrong person to perpetuate your ideas."

"I've got a coupon you might be interested in."

"From Lucky Strike? Congratulations." His voice sounded relieved. "You may speak in front of the Council."

"I thought this was the Chamber of Commerce."

"I'm redirecting you to the City Council."

So, Tampa was to become a smoke free city in Paul's eyes. Florida was to boast of leadership in cultural awareness, a political rarity. The red and blue state was finally joining the union. And Paul had a job. He was to be the social advocate who pushed Mad Mothers to second rank. He was to be the Puff Adder, the swelling spokesman who undid the tobacco industry. He was to be the quintessential spokesperson of a tobacco free Florida.

But he did not want the job. Although it was well paid from contributing sources— mostly clean-breasted chaps, he could not stand the prospect of enduring the repetition needed, i.e., the repeating of harangue after harangue on a single topic. Why be any more controversial than he was? Why stop smoking actually? Just because your lungs collapse and you can't breathe? It was an infringement on the first amendment right and the pursuit of happiness.

No, he would not hawk the message. He would not force anybody to do anything. Life without tobacco is painful. Oh, those first couple of years of withdrawal. Not to mention the next ten as well. He would not quit even if the price were right.

To be honest, he was torn: get paid as a promoter of health or continue to smoke uninhibitedly.

The more Paul thought about it, the less inclined he was to promote any program, but he had made an appointment with the council and would keep his commitment.

Somewhere, the gods smiled.

Tick tock went the timer.

The Council

He spoke before the council the following Monday.

"As you all know, Mr. Undres is here to address us on the benefits of a smoke free city. No municipality on the East coast has a program quite like the one Mr. Undres proposes. We would all do quite well to listen to him. It would be a shining star for us in the sunshine state to be ahead of the times. I welcome Mr. Undres."

The silence that greeted him was deafening, but Paul Undress was unfazed.

"Hello… councilman… and council women," Paul spoke slowly, enjoying himself. "I'm here to propose we pass a law outlawing all tobacco products. The only way to kick the habit is to enforce our own beliefs on each other. A fine equivalent to a DUI would do nicely."

His eyes were ablaze. "I've done some research. Preventive care is in. We would save roughly 100 million, which is nearly one-eighth our total revenue income here in Tampa. That's a big part of the pie chart. We could afford subsidized housing with that windfall. If not, I plan to go to bus stations and urban points of decay to sign up the masses for a petition to do what we could do here and now without all that trouble. Would you like to be a true dissident and accept my proposal as the only progressive thing to do?"

"Mr. Undres, like all proposals, we take it under consideration." The chairman added, "I want you to know there's a city ordinance against panhandling, and we consider petitions to be panhandling."

"I'll call Action News 8 then, and go viral." He felt a sudden rush of amusement at the whole thing.

"Give us a couple of days."

"You have two days."

Live Coverage

Two days elapsed. The Council refused to budge. If Paul were to make it a smoke free city, he would have to force an ordinance down their throats. Actually, the whole affair seemed worn out by now. It was okay if he smoked. And others? It was their right. Had the law changed all that much in 2020? Was it illegal to harm yourself? If it was, then the penalties could number in the thousands, millions, and the revenue would more than pay for infrastructure. Aging bridges would once again be the archway to a happy motoring public. Coal burning plants wouldn't exceed proper air quality, nor should second hand smoke exist in any form. A corporation can't be liable, but an individual cigarette smoker can.

So the Council balked. He went to the panhandlers' newsletter office. He put in an article about the petition. On every street corner, every traffic inter-section, the message was propagated.

Soon, Action 8 News called. "Mr. Undres, we'll like to put you on the six o'clock news."

"Sure."

The camera crew and Gail Stem, microphone in hand, talked with him face to face, while the Fox News viewing public looked on. "Mr. Undres, I understand you're starting a movement. Tell us about it."

Paul beamed. "It's big."

"You want to ban smoking?"

"I want to ban the pleasure of smoking," Paul answered, giving her a shrewd smile. "You can smoke only if it hurts you."

The wide grin on Gail Stem's face faltered. "Ladies and gentlemen, there you have it. Mr. Undres, a smoke free advocate— a man of few words."

Paul waved his hand to the camera, flicked his butt on the ground, and slowly walked away.

The Goddamn Gods Again

Paul is selling the city out!

A bolt of lightning lit the sky somewhere in Tampa.

It's too late. Climate change is here to stay. It changes everything. The carbon dioxide from cigarettes is just another stimulus for disaster.

Paul says the market is ripe for nicotine chewing gum.

They'll never hire an old man as a smoke free advocate.

"He's only seventy-one— that's young. He may live to
be seventy-two. He also celebrated his AA birthday
last month.

Smoking will undo him, sobriety or no sobriety.

Let's cut to the chase. The dead know what they did
wrong. Let's hear from them..

We're discussing the living.

We all need the big picture.

We are the big picture.

Is it fair to say Paul deems life worth living as long as
he can smoke?

He lives for his cigarettes. I repeat, let's ask the dead
what they think about it. They deserve to be heard. It's
not all about us.

Hellish Retorts

Down below, the atmosphere was less congenial.

Paul is coming.

He'll upset the entire atmosphere here. We need
another existentialist, like a hole in our putt putt range.

He is no longer alienated. He's earning respect.

A ragged voice cut through the silence that followed
the statement. Let's create a thought that will mislead
him like his childhood adaptations did.

He saw old acquaintances at the high school reunion.

That's a start for the hell he's in.

We don't drink coffee down here.

*He has to quit the caffeine kick too. Coffee dehydrates
the body. More than our hell even.*

A glass of water would be nice.

A ghoulish look came over one of them.

Forget it. We don't have water down here.

Don't forget there's no pleasure down here either.

*That's the trouble with the gods. All they think about is
pleasure. Paul's figured this out, the folly of pleasure.
He's with us.*

He'd love to experience death first hand. It seems...

The gods are pulling for him.

Don't mention them again. They bore me with their presumption.

Don't say 'me.' You're nobody like the rest of us.

A squeaky voice croaked. Let's start with some coughing nails.

*Go ahead plant a few. He's inflaming public opinion
with his sore throat.*

Let's make room for him, guys.

We're totally anonymous, aren't we?

He'll fit in nicely.

Heaven Speaks Back

The voices echoed. Their syllables went through the air like leaves carried by a breeze.

It looks like Paul has the love of the dead.

They're rock solid down there. They say we're pernicious pleasure seekers.

The group shared a self-indulgent smile.

At least we have the rain.

What's the word on Paul? Here or there?

Let him choose. He's broadminded enough.

Yet he does have that inane relationship with Chilli.

Then there is Rufus, Waldo, Crazy Crow, and Scotty.

He calls himself a Twelve Stepper.

And a caregiver to his dysfunctional family.

He's due for an illness of his own.

He has the disease of alcoholism.
A drink would be just the thing to reverse his long climb toward respectability.

Let the underground concern themselves with that.

I want the author of the step series to be acknowledged alongside Bill and Bob.

A soft chuckle came from the rest.

Please.

The Unemployment Office

The high heavens and the low hells were on full alert. Paul had a low opinion of both institutions. He preferred the counterculture of earth, alive and well, here in America. It was a substantial and growing force ever since Viet Nam. Black Lives Matter. Defund the Police. There was more camaraderie in that earthy movement than the ruthless, uncaring institutions of heaven and hell.

He was an unknown, but not for long. His books would bare his peccadilloes and make him much appreciated as a scatologic. However, he would never spend a cent to market his books. He didn't appreciate the business aspect of selling his brand of humor.

Even though he had 100 percent VA, he felt inclined to go to the unemployment office. It was something to do. He wanted to check the job market. A call center was the only job left in computer America. The knowing helps the unknowing on devices and apps that man uses for cutting corners were in high demand. It was hard to keep up with all the graphics.

But before he applied, he had to get by the guards.

Yes, there were guards with guns at the employment center, just as there were at schools and airports and all federal buildings. He didn't want to go postal, because his presence might be interpreted as that of a troublemaker, a maladjusted misfit inclined to chaos since he didn't really want a job in the first place. A true job seeker might want to shoot up the place out of frustration or a depressed sort might bomb the facility because of rejection in the workplace.

In the old days, a guy could simply walk in and apply for a job and lie. Nowadays, a person's complete history is obtainable on the computer by companies prior to an interview. Deceit is out.

Employers like flaws, however. They know you have to be stupid to want to work. How had a nation, affluent in the sixties, graduated to such a condition? Which drug, which overdose, was responsible for such a condition?

The security guard started it. "Watch out for the shadow government, sir."

Paul looked at him. He hadn't started this conversation. "The shadow government? What's your take on it?"

The security guard fingered his holster, his voice coming out in gasps. "We have the worst president we've ever had."

"Why is that?"

"His tax returns." The man didn't blink. He gave Paul a long stare.

"Is he born again?"

"Maybe." The man jutted out his chin, protruded and contorted his mouth.

"Did the shadow people help him?"

"They did."

"These shadow people… are they around here?"

The guard fingered his holster again. This time, nervously. "God damn right."

"People like him. He can't think."

"He's a wheeler dealer. I hate him even though I'm a cop. Cops like him."

"Listen, officer… I'm infiltrating."

"What was that? Say that again."

"I gotta sneak out of here. Tell the vet rep I had no choice."

"Mr. Undres…" a voice called out. A man who looked like a vet rep suddenly appeared.

"How did you know my name?"

"We know everyone. You registered here twenty years ago."

"Ahhh."

Paul steadied himself with dizzying exertion and walked with the rep into the section of booths housing the other employment counselors inside the building.

"The guard outside seems overly protective."

"That's the nature of police. Now take this test."

After fifteen minutes, Paul got the results. He flunked the

psycho-social assessment quiz, a simple attitude quiz, for a banking job.

"It looks like the Bank of America job is out," the rep said.

"Did the psycho-social portray me in a bad light?"

"My contact wouldn't reveal the details."

"Now what?" Paul asked.

"Health care."

"Shit."

"I'm going to put you in an exchange." He plucked at the cuff of his shirt, smiling.

"This is disappointing. I had hedge funds and private equities all figured with the Bank of America job. I had planned to make big bucks."

"Pocket your dreams," the vet responded, raking his fingers through his hair.

Paul's forehead furrowed. "Health care is not my specialty. I'm sick of it."

"What better place to work?" When he continued, his voice was patronizing. "Get well. Go to the lobby and fill out the app."

"I'm walking out of here."

"Don't rile the guard," he replied.

"Wait, let's think this out. Fill out the app?"

"You need an app to fill out the app."

"Download one and get a virus?"

"Also make sure to write a cover letter."

"Let's do this tomorrow," Paul answered, shooting him a searching look.

The man took a long look at Paul. "Tomorrow's another day."

"That's your opinion."

"I'm sticking to it."

"The country is doomed according to the security guard," Paul said simply.

"We're here to apply for jobs, not question reality."

"How arresting! Is that a final judgment?"

"I can't say. HIPAA, you know. Be careful of what you say." The vet rep quickly glanced over his shoulder before whispering, "I think the workforce sucks personally.."

"That makes two of us," Paul said.

The Ecosystem

So, Paul was not going to get that cake job. Meanwhile, the ecosystem was suffering. He was not going to quit smoking while the ecosystem convulsed and gagged too. His disease seemed small potatoes in comparison.

But his lungs never felt better. All those premonitions! Fear that the suckers on the douche bags were becoming clogged was just that: groundless fear. Then, there was the apparition of another operation. Dr. Saw might screw up and let him die on the table. If he went to the VA, they would only be baffled at the X-rays and send him to a gynecologist.

Meanwhile, the environment cried out. Business like violations of nature were abominable. How could he best synthesize biotic and abiotic elements in nature to create pathways toward a green America? He was a homeopath. He wanted to treat the sicknesses with small doses so as to create immunity. Meanwhile, among the well, couldn't the living do anything more than procreate? Still, it would take only one little creature to change everything. The future belonged to it.

He got up and went to work on his own creations. He was writing again. He had his coffee, his smoke. He wrote that man's instincts were just that: primordial.

As to the Chilli, she was out and about. He closed his eyes, coaxing his mind to shut off visuals of Chilli's dancing. He slowly ran a finger over the keyboard while his mind wandered. Could Chilli get into shape? Was she ready to take his hand? She was a feisty one. He wanted to forge her street mentality into genteel aristocracy. Make her His fair lady. Unfortunately, she lacked the looks and the mentality.

Could he satisfy his life cycle with her? Like a black widow spider, she had bit him. He had flown head long into the coop. Did he have enough resilience for the poison she sowed? He was after all, a homeopath, given to small doses.

"Paul, I want to be your queen bee," she said.

"You're a fucking wasp. Pluck the stinger then," he said.

"I will when you come over…"

He stood up and made his way to the sink. Dousing his face with water, he chuckled.

Later in the day, she called again. "I brushed my teeth."

"Did the dentist give you some pain pills?"

"Please come and get me. I won't bite."

And so he did. Darin answered the door. "All I want is a little peace and quiet. You take her. I can't take it anymore."

"You guys need some food. You two haven't eaten in days." Paul stepped inside, overlooking the disarray of the apartment.

"I can't eat. I got the shakes," Darin said.

Paul shoved a hand into his pocket and handed some bills to Darin. "Here's some money."

"I'll take that," she said.

So, the bite took effect. He had forked over VA money to her boyfriend and, in turn, helped humanity as a giving human, a specie not given too much popularity in the ecosystem.

Synthetic Knowledge

Thus, two zen masters, Paul and Darin, were holding their cards awaiting the play when a highly charged woman— capable of taking both of them out with her fists— was needing a different game. The boys were just two hobby horses, and she was just in it for a rocking good time.

"Take what you can out of a relationship and put something back in it," Paul called out to Chilli's back while playing the heart card.

Chilli pivoted and raised an eyebrow, "I am what I am."

"You want to just be a taker?" Paul continued.

She quickly crossed the distance to where Paul sat and pointed a finger on his chest, jabbing softly. "Sounds good to me."

"Who are you fighting, Chilli?" Paul simply put it.

"All of you. Put up your dukes, Paul."

"Let's fight later. This is not a boxing match. I'm playing cards."
She didn't bat an eyelash. "I'm a realist. I've punched the numbers. Once

Darin dies, you can come and live with me. I'll give you half the house. He'll expire from malnutrition any day now."

"I will not!" Darin protested, throwing the ace of spades.

Chilli silenced him with a look and turned her attention back to Paul. "You're the Zen master. You know these things. In six more months, Darin and I are going to be broke because his inheritance will be exhausted."

"You both still have your monthly checks. The place is paid for."

"And?"

"You curb your appetite for crack… you're in."

"Wrong! We'll have just enough to pay for food and condo fees."

"What else is there?"

Chilli slowly brought her face close to Paul's. She slowly tilted her head so that her lips were mere inches from his ear. "Fun. Fun. Fun," she whispered.

"Fun is funny about living within your means." Paul said.

"Nothing lasts."

"Except eternity,," came the Zen Master's hollow reply.

"So?" she sneered. "I can't have God staring at me."

"Chill. Get a grip. Do you think He's going to steal your meds?"

She pointed a finger to the side of her forehead, rapidly tapping it. "They're stashed. He can't find them."

And so, the card game ended. Chilli's idea of fun was to land all three in jail. She could get physical and land them in jail on a domestic violence charge on top of a drug charge on top of violation of probation charge. The possibilities were endless.

Once a well-paid dancer, now simply a slut. Since sluts are used, beauty was hard to come by, but Chilli tried. Her inner beauty was a muscular, twisted torso. She owned a part of Darin, and she owned part of Paul. Paul asked himself: would she ever become capable of recognizing the myriad forces at play from a physique so drugged?

Paul took her from Darin's to his place to quiet her nerves. Maybe sex would help. It didn't. It wasn't all that fun. He wasn't into just bodies. They got dressed. It was theirs to repeat if Paul desired. They had the rest of their lives to copulate. That was the physical reality.

"I need to renew my meds," she said. "My back is killing me."

Paul cleared his throat. "Want to listen to some music?"

"Sure." She manipulated the radio.

Paul quickly readjusted the dial.

"Want some coffee?"

"Sure."

"Have some of mine."

A cup of coffee, the car radio, and the hum of the engine were all they had as they went to Dade. Mania, bipolarity was the focus. Attention deficit disorder was in. Arriving, serotonin and dopamine agents were wearing holsters in the clinic. After the session, she came out. She wanted to celebrate her support system; she wanted to get high.

Paul's voice broke through her mental musings. "AA is a cult, Chilli. Its messiah is Bill Wilson. Would you like a Cult 45?"

She gave him a boisterous laugh. "Did you like all those microbial agents I gave you during our last tryst?"

"I don't care anymore. I like the part Dr. Silkworth mentions about 'synthetic knowledge' stating there are miracles beyond the knowledge of medicine and science.

The turning point for him had been the simple thought—why not die of VD—an idea so uncomplicated yet solved the complexity of diseases. He remembered the fizz of Pepsi Cola was as good as the bubbles of beer. That was as caloric as it got. Her brain needed a more complex solution. More pills, more booze, more crack, and more...sex.

Terminal Illness

Paul had grown up with four guiding lights— as a stepson to a stepfather, a real son to a real father, a real son to a real mother, and a stepson to his stepmother— yet he disobeyed them all. His childhood was spoiled by pets, animals that provided intimacy not normally given to pets. With such a foul start, it continued with a love affair with pot. LSD, PCP and crack. Like Chilli, he had stunted an imperfect beginning with a lousy finish.

He was now the undisputed oldest living member of the family. Competing members of his family assumed the oldest heir mantle was marginal despite his present drug free lifestyle. It wasn't enough to be merely clean, a man has to be squeaky clean for his upstarts.

Chilli, on the other hand, was all dirt. She worked frantically on tying frenetic pieces of self and crack into a perfect relationship, but there was always the driving need for more until sheer exhaustion set in, at which time blessed unconsciousness followed.

Cason had told Paul upfront that she was terminal, but Paul didn't see it. He saw a degree of love that no one else had for him.

He took her back to her home and went home himself. At her place, she used again, got beat up—this time by a sex client—suffering chest pains, neck pains, and back pains. If she wasn't terminal, what would you call it?

Maybe she could hammer out a few more highs before she went. Darin had promised her his house upon dying, but his aunt had other ideas. As the third member in the love triangle, he was not a fountain of strength with his twelve pack a day habit. He drank very slowly and moved equally so. He smoked too and already had one lung removed. He got around on crutches.

Like a carefully crafted diagram from Leonardo DaVinci's depiction of human anatomy, the pinpoints of nerve endings told the story. They were agents to pressure points firing off erratically, leading to haphazard behavior all around. The marriage ship was sinking fast.

A New Red Herring

The cat scan determined many things. The douche bags were doing their job, but they also were a seeding ground for infection. His workouts at the Y were warding off bronchial congestion, but a cancer was multiplying in the face of a tired immune system.

It was fundamentally funny that the transplants were causing cancer. That was why they were installed in the first place. The terminal triangle just got tilted once more.

There were several hidden meanings in all this. The red herring was that life was meant to be lived naturally, not mechanically and yet Paul was now a cyborg. The pleasure of good tobacco started with Sir Raleigh and extended from the Far Eastern trade routes to the New World as a vice, which, in the earlier part of civilization, pervaded all cultures and was accepted. But back then the average lifespan was not in the seventies for good reason..

Now the smoker was a pariah. In the new millennium, tobacco was taboo. Health reasons. Medical costs. Lost time in wages. Lost time in productivity. Loss of life. An anachronism, like Paul, deserved cancer just because he was so backward, He was definitely not out of date considering his new composition, however.

He could quit smoking at any time, couldn't he? He could reverse the process in short order. That was the most misleading lie of all,

No holocaust, no Armageddon, no book burnings would rob Paul of his pleasure. The curling swirl of smoke from his smokes were mesmerizing. The spilling of his guts in humorous books was to be his legacy, and these could be printed on demand, whether he lived or not.

The reddest red herring of all was the inflammation. Nobody knew that except the doctors and nurses, although many a patient thought they knew best in the face of a maskless mentality that ignored science.

Post-Operative Elation

The light hurt his eyes. Paul blinked. He heard a soft echo of footsteps. A soft voice called out, "Paul?"

His throat felt constricted. He swallowed. Paul's eyes remain fixed on the light. He laid on the table, unmoving.

"It's Dr. Saw. We need to replace those douche bags."

When he found his voice, he coughed, "They're dirty?"

"They're sensitive to X-rays. They're melting."

"I thought the fear of chemotherapy was the reason I had my lungs removed in the first place?"

"The CAT scan you took at the VA has caused a chemical reaction."

The glare from the overhead light bulb played like blue/black lighted moonbeams inside his head. He felt the opening of his chest, the probing of scalpel, and the cutting of tissue. He hoped Saw was following Da Vinci's diagram and not doing reckless exploration.

The office clock motioned mercilessly under the operation.

Tick tock.

He was approaching a bright white light. It indicated something far off.

Tick tock.

"Wake up, Paul."

Paul took a moment to steady himself. He felt fuzzy, fogged. When he gave his surroundings a cursory glance, he saw the old douche bags laying on the floor. A newer synthetic version not susceptible to chemical influence was pumping vital oxygen, oxygen that couldn't be summoned before. This one had a synchronized pump. God, he felt good.

Another operation, another chance at life. The bright white light dissipated.

"I'm awake." Paul donned his comfy jeans and shirt and asked,

"Do I owe you anything?"

"No, as usual. It's a gift."

He thought of the family estate he had almost missed out on. In the elation of being granted a new reprieve, he would again become an interested party in the goings on of his family. He would split time between being the caregiver of Hymie with Cason, Sunshine, Snotty, and Jell and the courting of his love of his life, Chilli Peppers.

He arched his back, his face radiated conviction. "Let's hit it, Chilli," he said to no one in particular. Hearing his own words, he felt betrothed.

The Powers That Be

Brain cells, once corrupted, never return to their original state, but they can be replaced by redirected synapses. He must remain sober. It was his only chance. The luxury of just one beer was off the shelf. That was the concept that carried Twelve Step programs to the height of their success. Drinking was not a moral issue but a chemical one. The Big Book calls on a higher power to enable the alcoholic to overcome the mental obsession, but to Paul, it was the inner power's job. And he was convinced inwardly not to touch a drop.

He uninhibitedly rejected liquor. Couldn't he do the same with tobacco?

The general election of 2020 would be TV's best years yet. Paul wanted to call up the news stations and blurt that an inside power was the key, but Republicans already knew that as they squeezed the lemon heads. The lout of the land identified with the rest of the nation's idiots, which was the reason for his popularity.

Why hadn't he thought of voting for Trump? Blowing smoke was in, after all.

Death Sentence

Chilli was sleeping off another bout. She had missed a whole series of AA meetings and political debates. A shower was out. Shaving legs was out. What was in was agoraphobia, which a week of sleepwalking had triggered.

"Chilli?"

"Yes," came the meek reply.

"You sound drowsy."

"I am."

"Do you feel like putting out?"

"No."

"Another day?" He replied, the muscles in his neck pulsating.

"Yes."

Who was left? There were not many. Rufus had disappeared off the face of the earth. Crazy Crow was bird shit. Waldo was wallowing.

He made one last try. "The sex we had wasn't bad."

"I'm asleep," she muttered. That was it. His pet project was in the dog house. He really didn't feel writing. Money management was his concern. Maybe he could buy a job. Ah, a pay to work scheme. After all, one had to pay for an education. Perhaps the missing key the poor so lacked was to have the rich pay them for making money. Wasn't that the way it was anyway? He took in a deep inhalation of tobacco. Ah, that 100 percent.

He had a deep affection for Chilli. Her life was more worthless than his. Did he hate what she was doing? He was not a misogynist. Nor was he a misandrist. He was a chip off the old block. His father was an alcoholic, and so was he.

It was an inside job, remember? He had been going to AA for years but was too mercenary to buy Chilli an engagement ring. How sober was that?

He took a long drag. Wisps of grey smoke curled in the air, lingering there for a brief moment before disappearing with the breeze.

Let's get the facts straight. He was a lonesome man, fundamentally happy at being alone. He would stick with Chilli because it was a death sentence and he, to no one's surprise, wanted to die.

Ersatz Extant Etc

Ersatz means a substitute, an inferior product from the original and is an adjective. Extant is about a surviving manuscript and is also an adjective Paul's book had it all. Ersatz, extant, etc. The substitute for reality was an artificial attempt at leaving behind something after his departure. The inner power had told him to put it down on paper. Another told him to make sense, sentence by sentence, paragraph by paragraph, chapter by chapter. If Paul was a madman, let the reader recoil.

Was there a substitute for living? Yes, a book that bespoke utter fantasy. A required reading for the appreciative mind. The real thing didn't matter anymore according to popular politicking.

The one ingredient that propelled him forward was tobacco. He had metabolized it. It was time to raise the bar a notch. Buy four packs a day instead of just three.

Chilli, Crazy Crow, Rufus, Darin, Waldo, Cason, Jell, Sunshine, Hymie, and Nutty: all invoked inconsequential association. He was only the recorder, the historian, the annotator extant of ersatz reality. Create a little cerebral happiness by confusing everyone.

The last place to look for immortality was an ersatz extant work of art. In it, there was no hidden truth, but there was the exposure of falsehoods. This was ersatz vision or extant screed. He could stay put next to his computer in his house and drive home his point, leaving extant an entire story without ersatz verbiage. Two words of which a whole chapter could be written.

Zen Grey

Paul looked at himself in the mirror. It was a most unpleasant visage. His face showed his age. Even though he had showered and shaved, he presented a countenance that was weather beaten. He took to the living room and lit up. He ran his tongue on his chapped lips, wetting them. Last night, he had found in two words the definition of obscurity. He would die of cryptic code. But enough of idle speculation, he had a woman to marry.

He left the keyboard and made ready to pick up Chilli. They both had made plenty of mistakes. Now was the time to gloss over them all and marry what was left.

He had been so close as a Zen master, but she had entered the monastery. She was the ultimate twelve step project, an example of what not to do. She was not a newcomer. She was a chronic relapser.

He would marry her to keep her quiet. The room grew quiet at that. He took a deep breath and closed his eyes as he sat cross-legged on the couch. He went into a deep, deep trance like the good monk he was.

Losing One's Head

Paul powered the Prius to Lake and Nebraska. The Parts Shack was rocking.

The blacks were having a party at the Chelsea Church next door. Paul knocked on the door of the Shack.

"Nurse Bite, so good to see you." Bite had a gleam in her eyes.

"Paul, you've gotten a lot of mileage out of one coupon."

Paul rubbed his arms, as though warming himself. Dr. Saw looked a bit manic. The man's vein seemed to be popping out of his neck as he spoke, "Lie on the table, Paul. I have a new head waiting."

"Sit, Paul," said Bite.

"Have some punch."

Paul swigged what appeared to be Kool Aid. Dr. Saw bent up over, hovering with a gas mask.

"Breathe, Paul."

"Paul," Nurse Bite whispered "Life is a bummer. Appearances being what they are, it's a shallow world. Dr. Saw is going to cut your head off."

Paul remembered his image in the mirror. "And put it in a jar?"

"It's not worth preserving," Saw said in a plummy voice.

"Please let me take it with me," Paul begged.

"You'll need a seeing eye dog after this."

"I love animals. I was just bored and wanted to talk to my spiritual advisor. I didn't expect to lose my head. By the way, I haven't had a punch that tastes this good in years."

The room changed. The walls fluctuated. Paul swooned; his head rested gingerly on the edge of the table. At least that was the way he saw it. The last he heard was, "Take him outside."

The sunshine was blazing. He had no wallet, no car keys. He was next to a bum at a green dumpster. All he could do was think for himself. He started walking. Step by step, he went to what he thought was the direction home. The spare key hidden under a potted plant was gone. The door to the house was ajar. Inside was a sense of violation. All his possessions were gone. His legs felt wobbly. He gripped the side of the bunk and slowly lowered his body to lay down. He lay on the bunk and stared at the top rungs of the metal bunk bed with empty eyes. Smoke came into the room, bringing with it a rancid odor. He breathed deep and felt for his head. Not finding it, he wondered what was next?

He opened his eyes. He was still on the couch, sitting cross-legged in a Zen position. He had gone nowhere. It seemed hours had passed. His head! He had one!

His computer was still there. It had never departed. The trusty word processor. His stereo waited patiently to be turned on. His car keys and wallet were on the coffee table. His head fit nicely on his shoulders. He knew this. Saw was not to be trusted, but he was his PCP, primary care physician.

Was his impending marriage causing stress?

He went to the man. "I'll take that tube you were talking about."

Saw looked at him strangely. "We didn't discuss a tube" he replied as he turned his back to Paul and picked up a chart. "

"Go ahead fit me anyway."

A sadistic smile disfigured Dr. Saw's thin lips. "Lie down, Paul."

The Tracheal Tube

So now he had a tracheal tube— douche bag lungs, replaced groin, and now this. Yes, both he and Chilli smoked, but how many artificial attempts towards stopping must he employ? They had in common tobacco usage. They breathed life into each other. He may be a Zen Master, hiding in concepts, but he now breathed in new life with the newly installed tracheal tube, inflaming her with hot air. Never had he awakened to a better ideology than what Dr. Saw espoused, refit everything. It was derisive allopathy, hardly a homeopath's way. It was a new talk show. He could communicate from his throat without moving his lips.

Would Chilli still be interested? Maybe he had gone too far. It appeared his focus on quick fixes was limitless.

It was Sunday. Time to see the folks again. It was such a long drive and such a short visit. Dad had a steak and salad all prepped and ready for cooking. Meet the Press and the NFL were to follow.

He had made a quick visit to Club YANA beforehand. The welcome was heartwarming and unexpected. The last time that had occurred had been in kindergarten. He felt like a kid. The reception was glowing.

"We hear you're going to get married. Congratulations."

Through his tracheal tube, he said, "thanks."

He thought of what Chilli had told him— he was scaring people away.

He ran his eyes over the crowd and asked, "Do I scare you, people?"

Everyone was afraid to look; his voice sounded funny.

The Cork Stopper

Not to be outdone, Paul submitted Chilli to Dr. Saw. Paul's skin was pasty and pallid. He didn't look the part anymore. He ran his hand down the arm that tightly gripped the steering wheel. His voice was barely audible over the sibilant noises of the engine. "Chilli, you're going to marry me."

"Oh, Paul. I've been waiting to hear those words for years. What will people say? That I'm a gold digger? That I overcharged my true john?" Her words came tumbling one after the other. She beamed at him.

"Once Dr. Saw rebuilds you, you'll make your husband proud. He is just the mechanic to grind you into shape."

"Do I need to buy a dress? Am I wearing the right outfit for Dr. Saw?"

"This is not a dress rehearsal, Chilli. It's a medical opportunity."

They arrived at the Body Shack. After a short exchange of pleasantries, Paul made his pitch. "I bring you my fiancé, Chilli Peppers. I want her to stop drinking."

Dr. Saw extended his hand. "Nice to meet you, Chilli. I've heard so much about you. I understand you're Paul's better half."

Chilli responded with a half shrug and asked, "How's my head?"

"You can keep it."

Chilli pirouetted and bowed. "Do you like my new outfit?"

"Smashing," he replied.

Chilli looked at Paul then back at Dr. Saw. "I hope you're not going to spell out some AA bullshit."

Dr. Saw produced a tumbler of whiskey. "Drink, it'll be your last. You're susceptible to alcohol, but I have just the thing, Chilli."

"Anything physical, doctor." Chilli said.

"I see you're tattooed and pierced. This is going to be a breeze. Lie down, girl."

"Her heart is in the right place," Paul ventured.

"Relapse is just too tempting, hey?" Dr. Saw bent over Chilli's limp frame. With a pair of tongs, he inserted a cork stopper down her throat.

"Will the stopper work? Nothing else does." Paul asked.

"It'll bottle her up."

"But will it uncork her?"

Dr. Saw scratched his chin and was quiet for a brief moment. Then, his voice boomed, "I'm not her sponsor."

The Pros and Cons of Marriage

Chilli was cured. She would never drink again. That was just the solution Paul was looking for. He was cruising in the Prius listening to hip-hop now because of her. The driving sound in his car transmitted his enthusiasm for the big day. The gods chose to insert a few bars.

Do you think Paul has the right approach

He sees a doctor of atheistic inclination.

But as to Chilli, he needs to woe instead of wow.

*It doesn't take much to woe or wow Chilli. Twenty
bucks usually does it.*

The morning after pill goes for fifty.

That's on her.

He doesn't love her. It's nothing more than a death wish.

*He does love her. She's the only one that bugs him. He
wants to support her since he was given that free ride
by the VA. He has to buy something with all that VA money.*

What about a stroke

"He can't buy that.

Tick tock.

Paul was merrily obvious to their chatter. He was rocking to the car's radio. He was with his girl.

He simply can't keep smoking and expect a robust life.

He has to make a choice. Life with Chilli or death by

tobacco. Let's make him a pauper where he can't

afford to smoke.

"It doesn't stop the homeless.

Still oblivious to their chatter, Paul leaned over the car seat and kissed Chilli. "Let's do it."

"I've been thinking, Paul. I can't leave Darin. He's dying and has written me in his will. I get his house. You can move in. But not now. You'll have to wait."

"I thought…" He paused in mid-sentence, sorting out his disappointment.

"I want to share my life with you. The moment Darin dies—"

The Day Darin Died

Darin died. He OD'd on sheer exhaustion. His Zen had zapped. Paul's phone rang. An excited voice came through the airways. "Paul! Darin's dead."

"Keep your head. Call 911. Don't get rid of the body. It was an accident, right? You didn't hit him, did you?"

"I didn't touch him. It's unreal, he's dead! We can get married!"

"Did you cause it, Chilli?" Paul pressed.

"I don't think so. I was in a blackout."

"I'll be right over."

"Hurry."

Paul sped to Chilli's. The paramedics were just leaving. He immediately asked Chilli what was up.

She shook her head, looking perplexed. "The paramedics resuscitated him. He's alive as ever."

When Paul didn't say anything, she spoke in softer tones. "Truthfully, I thought we had our wedding present."

A half hour later, they walked into the 301 AA clubhouse. The topic was God's will. Chilli spoke compulsively. "My name is Chilli, and I'm an alcoholic and drug addict."

"Hi, Chilli," came the chorus.

"I don't want to go to jail. I can't drink anymore. Dr. Saw put a stopper in my throat. Every time I did drink, I blacked out and hit people. I've attacked my mother and my father. I've attacked the cops. I've even attacked by boyfriends. One of my boyfriends almost died at my hands this morning."

"We thought Paul was your boyfriend."

"I love them both."

"You can't have it both ways, Chilli."

"Yes I can. I do it all the time both ways."

But the wisdom of the rooms prevailed. Chilli could not have it both ways.

The Day Chilli Died

Darin was not dead. yet. Chilli was. She had OD'd on vomit. Darin called Paul. "My girlfriend is dead. What do I do?"

"Give her a kiss goodbye."

"She's got puke all over her face."

Ten minutes later, there was another call from Darin. The paramedics, the much heralded first responders, had pumped her back to life. The paramedics were becoming quite a nuisance. Chilli had opened her eyes.

"Don't you think she should have her stomach pumped?" Darin asked.

"Give her a laxative."

"I'm calling the cops."

"Why?"

"She hit me."

"You'll both go to jail on domestic violence. It'll be a VOP on her and a domestic violence charge on you."

"It doesn't matter the paramedics are taking her to the hospital"

An hour later, Chilli called Paul from Tampa General. "Come pick me up. They cleared my throat of the stopper. I feel like a meeting."

"Are you dressed for it?"

"No," she replied without hesitation, "take me to Macy's first."

Paul drove down to Tampa General. Chilli was out of ICU and waiting in the parking lot. "Are you going to let me in the car?"

"Give me a chance to unlock the door," he responded tartly. For a full instant, he felt fully depleted. "Can't you wait? I'm tired of this drama.". Either you or Darin just die and not come back. It's pure theatre. Let's go to your club instead of mine once again."

So, at the 301 House, the only smoking AA clubhouse in the city, Chilli lit up and said to the fellowship, "Hi, group, I just OD'ed. No joke, I'm serious as a heart attack."

The room was quiet.

"And?" one speaker asked.

"As a pill hound, I barfed and choked on my own puke."

One suggested that she gives him the rest of her pills.

"I don't share my drugs," she said.

"We're sorry about that, Chilli. You know everyone intimately in this room, What do you want, a little consoling? You are constitutionally unpopular."

Paul abruptly stood up. "A boomerang kills as effectively as the straight arrow. I think this whole affair is kangaroo. Do I have to go to Australia to marry her? Chilli has done a fifth step and confessed her shortcomings to the group. It's a big step for her."

"If you say so."

Proposing

"Chilli, are we on or off?"

"For what, actually?"

"You unfeeling bitch. Matrimony."

She jolted upright. "Do you trust me?"

"Of course not."

"I can pay my own food and rent. That way, I can pay back all those coffees you bought me as my dowry. "

Paul cut her off, holding a finger to his lips. "I want to get rid of my futon mattress and have it replaced with a Posturepedic. I want us to sleep right. I'll pay a house cleaner to come in and mop the floors. Take you out for all our meals. Those are the minor adjustments. You'll be very happy listening to my car stereo and cruising with me. As long as I can take you to your pain specialist and shrink's office, not to mention the prescription store, you'll be happy. You will essentially place your entire life, as shallow as it is, in my hands."

"That's right. I just want to be serviced, please Paul."

And there it was again— that honeyed voice Paul had come to know so well.

"You want me to make up for all my wrongs with one fell swoop?" She leaned forward, towards him. "Kiss me."

No sooner had she uttered those words than Darin died for the last time, and they were free to marry at last.

A Sleep Number Bed

Paul got a deal on mattresses and purchased a Sleep Number bed instead of a Posturepedic. The price was beyond his usual two cents but was well worth it. Anything for Chilli, the insomnolent one.

She was, at heart, sensitive. The tough facade belied a little girl crying for help. She was amusing. What assets would a broken back and a snapped neck bring to the mattress? Paul was not exacting, quite lenient, as a matter of fact. He had his adjustable side, and she had hers.

Meanwhile, a firm mattress meant a firm foundation for the would be newlyweds.

Dream Drifting

In all the annals of Paul's life, this marriage was the cake in forsaking good judgment in getting kicks. He hadn't really mined the full depths of depravity with Chilli. He hadn't really gotten involved in her scene in a deep personal way. He had always helped from a distance. She did like older men, of which he qualified. She wasn't forcing herself on him. This idea was apparently all Paul's. She just wanted assurance that Paul was committed to giving her something back other than scorn.

While Paul mulled all this, he went into a troubled sleep the day before the wedding.

Life drifted like waves. His real father held the helm of a sea tossed shrimp boat. Paul was the shrimper as in the first mate. They were the only two on the boat. The storm was horrific. He had headed enough shrimp for a full load. He was chillin' now. Better to ride out the storm in the bunk.

The gods looked on.

Paul seems to be dreaming.

He has reached the pinnacle of manhood, a storm-tossed shrimper.

He needs to take his dreams seriously.

The storm picked up. Forty-foot waves sloshed overboard. The boat was awash. The netted shrimp scattered like bugs. The captain disappeared. Paul felt the water flood his small bunk. The boat went down with a gigantic gurgle.

Giant squid feasted on the cargo. A sperm whale rammed the vessel. Despite the distractions, Paul remained calm. He had an oxygen tank. His douche bags drunkenly sucked the air in. A mermaid with the face of Chilli wiggled enticingly outside.

Paul seems oblivious to the implications.

He's as hard headed as she is. Will his experience as a twelve stepper be sufficient to get him out?

Chilli has seen hardship that rivals the most desperate
of recovery seeking girls. She has some swimming to do.

All he and she need is to stand firm for something they
believe in. Paul has the hash filled days of Morocco;

Paul's dream persisted. He grew tired of looking at the mermaid and donned some flippers. He left the vessel, now cradled precariously on a ledge of a much steeper deep-sea precipice. As soon as he exited, the craft went over, disappearing into the deep.

He swam seemingly forever to the top. The storm abated. The bright sheen of the surface reflected the moon's luminosity.

He paddled for hours, staying afloat until the Coast Guard spotted him. They took him aboard. The captain of the rescue vessel was his father again.

"Dad, you get around."

"I had to leave the shrimp boat by the helicopter in order to save you."

"Thanks, Dad, you really shouldn't have."

"It's because I love you, son."

The words echoed as a tsunami barreled towards them.

Paul awoke drenched in a sweat. He was having trouble breathing. The douche bags were filled with water. He barely made it to the Parts Shack.

"These bags...Dr. Saw...

"I'll just pump your chest. There you go."

"How come my body doesn't reject them?"

"They're as inanimate as you are."

"I want some waterproof ones."

"Let's do it."

The procedure went well. Paul drifted in another trance-like state.

The shrimp boat came to the surface. The damage by the sperm whale was minor. Paul took the helm. His father stood by him.

"Dad, why isn't love for me?"

"Some people aren't destined for the true thing, son."

"Wake up, Paul." A commanding voice said..

"Whoa, I'm awake. I've been dreaming about a fucking shrimp boat. My father is trying to tell me something." Paul looked apprehensive. "I think I should think twice about this marriage."

"How's Chilli?"

"She's weird. She's sad. She's afraid. She's touchy. Let's just say that she's challenged. Like any older man, I love a young thing. It'd be nice if she was a good lay for all her experience."

"You need her."

"Coming from you that makes me laugh."

"You think I'm just a body trafficker. In reality, I'm simply an expediter. We're all unique—different— Paul."

"Don't you mean 'difficult?' If it hadn't been for Chilli, I would never have gotten a semblance of manhood that you provided. For the last twelve years, I've been celibate. I'd have gone through another twelve- or thirteen-years making amends and never touching another woman. I owe her the thrill of being with and having a woman."

"Give me a cliché I can cling to," Paul added.

"Keep on, keeping on."

"And another?"

"Smoke 'em if you got 'em."

The Finale: Face First

The wedding was at Paul's parent's house. Cason did the ceremonies. In addition to being a board-certified attorney, he was a licensed marriage broker. Paul did an assessment of the guests. They were all Cason's NA friends who just liked the opportunity to spend time on the beach. They all toasted well wishes with lemonade and soft drinks.

"Do you, Chilli, pledge to be there for Paul no matter what?"

"I do."

"Do you, Paul, pledge to be there for Chilli no matter what?"

"Naturally."

"Until the end?"

Tick Tock.

A bolt of pain hit Paul's chest. His legs went limp, and he went down on his knees, falling face first on the sand. His mind went blank. The back of his head blew up, sending goblets of brain throughout the crowd. His face burned an exact image of it in the sand, a glassy portrait that radiated steam.

"He flatlined," Chilli cried, falling over the corpus.

Cason pulled out his cell phone from his black clothed cloak. "We have an emergency here at Gulf Blvd."

The paramedics came, but Paul was dead. It was a ruptured douche bag that caused an aneurysm in the head. The root cause? Tobacco.

Paul had finally quit smoking.

In the casket, Paul wore a translucent garb. His soul was impeccable. The dog of doggerel had chewed his last tidbit. The master of wit had been blown away.

Paul has made it.

A crisp breeze carried the voices.

How do you feel, Paul? We use first names up here.

Not too bad. Got a cigarette?

You're dreaming, Paul.